MW01251404

Mage's Mistake

Book Four of the Tales of Menel Fenn

By K.D. Nielson

Other books by KD Nielson

The Lich War Series

Amberwine

Cassandra of Cr' Mere

A Line in the Sand

Tales of Menel Fenn

Osey

Fool's Quest

The Confederation Kingdoms of Bree

Mage's Mistake

Ghost Dancer

DSMR Series

Through The Portal

Copyrighted K.D. Nielson 2012

* * *

All rights reserved. Without limiting the rights under copyright reserved above, no part of this publication may be reproduced, stored in or introduced into a retrieval system, or transmitted, in any form, or by any means (electronic, mechanical, photocopying, recording, or otherwise) without the prior written permission of both the copyright owner and the above publisher of this book.

This is a work of fiction. Names, characters, places, brands, media, and incidents are either the product of the author's imagination or are used fictitiously. The author acknowledges the trademarked status and trademark owners of various products referenced in this work of fiction, which have been used without permission. The publication/use of these trademarks is not authorized, associated with, or sponsored by the trademark owners.

* * *

Dedication

This book is dedicated to my loving and long suffering wife, Anita. The countless hours I drafted her into helping me are truly appreciated.

Also I would like to thank Debs, a kindred spirit who untiringly read the many versions.

The last person I would like to thank is Dale Caroline Russell for her input to my books and for writing the back cover write-up.

Covers designed by Amanda L. Matthews @ www.mandematthews.com

Prologue

The woman moaned sleepily and dragged her arm over her eyes, shielding them from the intrusive persistent light that sought to end her peaceful drowsy slumber. Finding that didn't work, she sighed and harrumphed loudly, swiftly dragging her pillow over her face and pulled the down comforter higher. For a brief few minutes, peace and tranquility reigned supreme and then, suddenly it was shattered as the covers were thrown back, and the woman levered herself upright, moaning grumpily, the quilt at her waist. With another irritated groan, she pulled the disheveled mahogany tresses off her face. Using her fingers for a crude comb she quickly dragged them through the long silken curls sorting her hair into some kind of presentable state.

She looked blearily around, her face slowly changing, reflecting the confusion she began to now feel. The woman swung her long shapely legs from under the covers, and lethargically pushed herself upright, automatically pulling down the long nightdress, straightening it from where it bunched up around her thighs. Her brow furrowed in concentration as she struggled to remember where she was, or even who she was. Suddenly the woman spotted something that registered with faint familiarity to her questioning mind, a long heavily tasseled pull cord. More confident now, she pulled it. Deep in the house she could hear a melodic chime. The woman waited expectantly for a few minutes. Soon she could wait no longer as her bladder demanded urgent attention. She bolted from the room; flung open the double doors and hurried along the second floor landing to another room. She stopped, sighing in relief, and turned the handle. However, the door wouldn't budge. She rattled the door, trying to dislodge it.

She cast about quickly and seeing two more doors on this level, hurried with all the dignity she could manage. She frantically tried the next door, it too refused to co-operate and she swiftly sped to the next, but it also remained firmly shut. She ran hastily down the wide grand staircase and paused uncertainly at the bottom; she could see three doors, and with an unladylike shuffle headed for the first. It opened into the dining room, the second, into some kind of library and the third opened outside. She gasped in dismay and desperately

5

cast about, seeing only one answer to her dilemma. She sprinted for the roses growing along the side of the house.

The young woman hurried through the garden casting furtive glances about, trying to determine if anyone witnessed her previously embarrassing situation. She hoped fervently that there was someplace where she could wash her hands, hurrying through the open door and stopped in flabbergasted bewilderment. The hourglass shaped grand staircase had literally been repositioned, or had it? She was reasonably sure the stairs had been side on when she had hurried down them a short time ago. Now, the polished wood, red-carpeted stairs filled the elegant foyer, and climbed gracefully to the second level. She could see the stylish classical wall-mounted glass lighting fixtures, tastefully positioned around the entry foyer. The woman shook her head seeing the round table secreted discreetly off to the side. She could make out a pewter pitcher and porcelain basin sitting on the polished oak, a carefully folded towel draped conveniently nearby. The woman stared at the table; she was positive that it wasn't here earlier. A little concerned, she carefully tiptoed forward, looking suspiciously from side to side, as her nightdress buffeted by the wind through the open door, molded her trim figure, the autumn-colored leaves swirling playfully about her legs. She carefully craned her head forward, holding her swirling hair off her face, and looked into the pitcher. A clear liquid shimmered in the wall-mounted lights, it was simply water. She picked up the towel, the whole situation was spooky, and she looked about warily.

As she slowly climbed the stairs, she ran her hand over the smooth, highly polished wood. The young woman could smell the oils used to varnish the oak; it reminded her of pine trees. Reaching the top, she paused on the landing and glanced apprehensively at the other doors off the hallway. The door closest to the top of the stairs was ajar. Curiosity overcame her concern when she saw the entrance, which moments ago didn't exist. She moved slowly, suspiciously, to the opening and peered in. The young woman blinked in disbelief, it was an indoor toilet. Panic hovered uneasily close by, why wasn't it there before?

6

The mahogany haired beauty stopped abruptly in the middle of her bedroom gaping at the room. She whimpered and darting past the perfectly made bed and the gorgeous dress, carefully laid out, over the back of an overstuffed settee. She fumbled frantically with the lever handle on the double French doors, and pushing through the sheer curtains clinging like spider webs to her face, hurried onto the balcony. There was a covered walkway to the left that ran along the short outside wall of the entry foyer, and turned and continued along the front of the house. In panic, she fled down the wooden terraced balcony, past the comfortable bench swings and reaching the turn, she stopped abruptly leaning against the railing gasping for breath. Her confused mind grappled with the events of the morning. This building was, in some parts, a copy of the house, where? Suddenly, she didn't know, she clenched her fist in frustration unable to remember anything. But how could things change each time she entered a room? It was as if the very house was alive and reading her thoughts. The young woman was truly troubled now. The memory of her past was like something glimpsed out of the corner of her eyes and disappearing when she turned to look directly at it. She inhaled deeply, steadying her pounding heart, her gaze wandered over the lush gardens covering the grounds. She could see small swing benches that were spaced about the ground, most positioned conveniently under big apple trees. The idea returned with more force; these gardens were just like the estate that she grew up in. That knowledge frightened her, and the woman focused on her childhood. She closed her eyes concentrating furiously. Nothing … as hard as she tried, she couldn't remember anything.

"Hello the house!"

The woman jerked upright, her wide staring eyes looked frantically about, as the voice echoed through the halls behind her. She looked around, suddenly terrified. There was no place to run. She made a herculean effort to calm down, why would the house be talking to her? She screwed her eyes tightly shut, and rubbed her furrowed brow; logically, someone else must be in the house.

"Anyone home, the front door was open, and no one answered my knock?" the unseen speaker called out again.

The woman's heart was pounding, her breasts heaving.

"Don't be stupid, calm down. There will be some rational explanation for all this." She jumped at the sound of her own voice, but strangely, it also calmed her.

She quickly recovered her poise as some instinct took over. She looked quickly at her attire and squirmed, she still wore her nightdress. Gathering her hem, the woman ran as quickly as decorum allowed, back to her room. As she stumbled through the clinging curtains, she could hear the measured tread of footsteps on the stairs. Strangely enough, she felt in control now. She shook her head, how could she have let her imagination run away with her? Now, more concerned with the proper etiquette for meeting her guest, she quickly shed her nightdress and grabbed the beautiful gown.

The footsteps stopped outside her door, and she could hear the discrete knocking on her partly open bedroom door. "Anyone here?"

She fumbled with the fasteners on the back. "Can you give me a minute?"

"Certainly, I was beginning to wonder if you were home. I began to despair you might have left the Sanctuary before I could get here."

She stopped shrugging into the dress, pulled half way up over her hips. That sounded rather ominous. She looked at the mirror in front of her. Her mind no longer rebelled seeing her reflection, standing half naked, in something that wasn't even in the room when she fled panic stricken only moments before. The woman finished buckling the wide belt across her shapely hips, and quickly checked herself in the mirror. She looked presentable, but then she noticed a small blue felt covered box sitting on the table behind the chair her gown had been draped on. She frowned slightly, she would check on it later. Now, sufficiently prepared she turned to the door.

"Come in."

The door opened, and with a tiny shriek her world went black.

* * *

The woman lay quietly on the bed. As her eyes fluttered she felt a damp cloth on her forehead. She reached for the towel, and could hear a cultured, pleasant voice, the language common, but spoken with the most charming accent she had ever heard. The

8

woman rolled to her side, and grasped the wet fabric as it slipped. She uttered a small gasp, and her bewildered mind fought the urge to faint again.

"There, you go my little friend. You like that don't you?"

She opened her eyes again slowly, and gawked at the man-sized frog feeding a little bird perched on his hand. He wore long black pants with two entwined gold stripes running down the outside leg, a white ruffled shirt, a black string tie and a short jacket made of black velvet, richly embroidered with gold thread. He had a wide, delicately tooled leather belt, splendidly decorated with spaced jewels upon which hung a finely crafted, if rather flimsy blade. His wide brimmed hat with a two-inch silver/turquoise band had a long sweeping feather discretely attached; lying on the settee next to him. He sat with one leg crossed on the opposite knee; the knee-high hard boots had a three-inch fold back near the top, and were like the rest of the man's attire, exquisitely detailed with rich patterns, carefully tooled into the highly polished leather. What made the whole situation so bizarre was the pleasant well-spoken voice came from the wide flabby mouth, and the bulbous eyes of a common pond frog, were fixed on the little yellow bird that picked greedily at the small lump of bread the creature held in his other hand. The young woman moaned again, and rolled onto her back, closed her eyes and replaced the damp cloth.

"Ahhh, you have recovered." He stood and bowed, with a flourish of sweeping hands said, "Let me introduce myself, I am Count Alex Richmond dan Ture. You may call me Alex, or Count if it is easier."

The woman's mouth moved, but nothing came out. Her mind still struggled with Alex's appearance.

"You still have the memory sickness," he said sympathetically.

Instant alarm flashed across the woman's lovely face, and her hands hastily reached for her cheeks.

The man/frog laughed, a rich pleasant sound. "It is not a real sickness; it is more of a readjustment the mind makes to what has happened."

"Just what has happened, and where are we?"

The man sat down, and the little bird hopped back onto his arm. "In your case, the logical answer will sound a bit harsh at first, but rest assured that you are safe now."

The woman relaxed slightly at his words. "I vaguely remember a long dark hall, filled with some strange grey mist, or light. There was some kind of a disturbance. I am not sure what happened?" she looked down, and touched her stomach just below her breast. "I remember something sharp stabbing me."

Alex nodded compassionately. "That's right. You were in what magicians call the Shadow Plane; it is a grey abstract version of the real world. It has its own laws, and physical properties."

She blanched and swayed. Alex was by her side steadying her. She didn't even see him move.

"I died." Her voice was little more than a hoarse whisper.

"Yes, you did. But with the condition of things at the time, you were sent here before your body's life essence truly diminished."

"What else can you tell me?" she flared angrily. "You seemed to know an awful lot about me! How do I know you weren't the one who killed me?"

Alex wilted under her harsh words, the big eyes fixed unblinkingly on her. "My dear, I have been here for a thousand years." He waved his hands at the surrounding house. "I too have a Sanctuary. However, I have been able to manipulate the 'stuff' this place is made of. I was a man of great power once, and after coming here, I have learned a thing or two, shall we say. I am able to know when someone arrives here, where they are and with a little extra effort, I am able to obtain certain answers."

The woman looked shrewdly at Alex, she was almost positive he was lying to her. Well, maybe lying was too harsh a word, but he wasn't telling her everything.

He went on, "I can tell you your name is Justina Ashworth. I will let your mind tell you the rest when it is able."

She mulled the name over in her mind; she suddenly remembered something, and looked intently at the blue box on the duchess. She quickly scooted to the side of her bed, and reached the bureau in three steps. Her quivering hands carefully opened the lid. The case was made of some kind of rock, and the lid was heavy as she lifted it away from the bottom. Inside she could see a small

10

jeweled crown, delicately made in silver, with gold flecks artfully spread about the beautiful filigree. It would have taken a master jeweler months to make the crown she now quietly lifted with trembling fingers. Impulsively she turned, and faced the mirror and gently lowered the crown on her head. Alex discreetly wiped away the tear that threatened to escape.

"It was specially made for you." He coughed to rid himself of the sudden lump in his throat.

Justina turned to question him more, but he was already on his feet, was reaching for his hat.

"I have to go; there are two other stops I have to make."

Suddenly, she was terrified at being left alone, even the malformed creature before her was company. She uttered a single sob, and she stepped forward impulsively reaching out for the man.

Alex automatically took her hand with both of his; his top hand caressed the woman's. He hastily stepped back when he became aware of what he was doing and with a flourish, put his hat back on. She looked in wonder at the man. His touch almost seemed familiar.

"You will be safe here. This house will cater to your wishes. Do not leave the marked grounds; the other Sanctuaries are not as pleasant to deal with."

"What of you? You have told me nothing of how you came to be here, what happened to you?"

"That my lady, will be a topic for a later time."

* * *

The Elven Sanctuary

The morning sunlight filtered through the massive yew trees to gently caress the ground. The small group of marble buildings glistened white in the early dew. Lush plants and exotic flowers grew in plentiful abundance. The different structures were definitely elven, High Elven to be exact. The spacious ceilings allowed the cool breeze in through the almost non-existent walls. Grouped columns, some close together, formed an impression of seclusion. Once inside, carefully placed panels, more foliage and bright flowers were spaced amidst displayed trophies, giving the appearance of separate rooms.

In once such room, a single padded chaise lounge occupied the center. A man, tall and well developed, lay as if asleep, his hands folded across his stomach. He would have been over six foot, but then most of the fairy races were, his blond shoulder length hair spilled out over the small oblong pillow. The face was handsome, almost pretty. The fine sculptured features were relaxed in *ess-tay*, the elf equivalent of sleep. An elf, no matter the race only needed a few hours of inactivity to renew their energy. The man's mind, already at work, registered the absence of the morning song that made Vanwa Hir one of the more pleasant lands to wake up in. The brow furrowed in concentration trying to discern why the absence of the birds bothered him. He was on the verge of ending the meditation trance when the familiar trill of the sweet sound wafted gently to him. His features softened and he relaxed. He did ponder why his highly disciplined mind was lacking in a few details. Again he went through *Leen-odd Nimm Bare-ehth*, the Song of the White Queen. He went through the formalistic ritual dedicated to his patroness, the Unicorn Queen. The words of the thirty stanzas came easily to his mind. This work was the first thing the acolytes learned. It had taken him five months to learn, then another four to integrate the singsong rendition in his daily life. From prayers over the dead, to greeting an opponent in battle, they even ended the day with the *Fay-ah Lehn*, literally wishing them a safe spirit journey. Now, using his training, he went through the song, the words once started came

12

unbidden to him, and by the time he had finished, there were few gaps left in his memory.

He lay as if dead, he remembered everything, his noble quest to banish evil from the land. He had formed a troop with his closest friends and retainers, even his younger brother, Coireall. They had sought a fabled sword; one that according to legend was powerful enough to kill even the greatest demon. However, to everyone's dismay, the sword turned out to be a demon lord, imprisoned within the blade. Before the night was over, Devron slew everyone but his brother, who had managed to wrest the blade from his grasp, and then, shattered the blade on a stone. But, the damage was done. The High Elf paladin grew darker, as the foulness from the blade was left to rot and fester. Now, that the demon lord was dead, Devron looked for something else to fill that resounding void. In the end, he found the drow witch elf, Naidor. She taught him, along with her daughter Laoise, all the dark arts she knew. Devron led an attack on his former homeland. The fighting was bitter. Hundreds of high elf men, women and children were killed, even his beautiful sister. The thousands of drow warriors that died were unimportant. His wounds had been serious, and as he languished near death he became preoccupied, obsessed with searching for the secrets of extending his life beyond this realm, eventually finding it in the dark arts. With a dedication that bordered on religious fanaticism, he devoted hours to making a special sacrificial knife that would end his mortal life and grant him immortality, in the form of a lich.

The man on the divan slid to the stone floor, his mind wracked with pain. He stumbled to his feet, and with an animalistic howl, fled the room. He ran blindly, his feet taking the path they had traveled thousands of times in the past, to the small temple. Here, he flung himself at the feet of the ten-foot marble statue. The beautiful woman knelt with her hands out-stretched, reaching for whoever knelt here. Devron threw himself at her feet.

"Nimm Bare-ehth, forgive me," he wailed. "I ask for your forgiveness," he shrieked. He cringed dejectedly as the rest of the memory of his past, rushed in on him; leading the attack on Justina's people, his cursing the daughter with vampirism, the fight with the dracon protector, his own disastrous defeat at the guardians hands.

13

Devron cringed at the statue of his patron as he remembered the confrontation with Bolinor and his wife Cassandra, the quest for the fire rubies to power the artifact. He rent his white tunic with the long scalloped sleeves and the white pants. He smashed his head onto the marble feet, and then staggered and fell, crashing heavily onto his back. He had split his head open, almost to the bone.

Devron looked up as a blinding light filled the room. He wiped the blood from the savage cut, and blinked at the woman he could see kneeling beside him. Her face was familiar and the elf furtively glanced sideways, to see an empty marble stand where the statue once stood. He looked up with reverent awe at the woman. Her face radiated an unearthly beauty, and the dazzling gown, seemed to be made of thousands of tiny stars covering her exquisitely formed body. The material was translucent, and she shimmered and glowed with a soft aura. He hungered for her, not for her tastefully displayed womanly charms, but her grace and her presence.

"Nimm Bare-ehth, is that you?" he levered himself up to see her.

The woman nodded. "Yes. I am with you. I have never left you. I was there all those years. You were one of my, *Har-mah*, one of my treasures. I would not abandon one such as you."

"Please, blessed Nimm Bare-ehth, take my life as payment for what I have done."

She shook her head; the beautiful long hair softly caressed his stricken face. Slowly he became aware that the pain had gone. He stupidly put his hand to his forehead. The blood and the gory gaping wound were missing.

"If you truly repent, I have a task for you." Her timeless voice caressed his tortured soul.

Impulsively Devron reached out and grasped her arm, peace flowed through him. "Blessed, Nimm Bare-ehth, I want to return to your presence more than anything. I will dedicate what is left of my miserable life to atone for what I have done. Please, Nimm Bare-ehth, forgive me!" he cried out in supplication.

"There is a woman, some miles from here. To gain my forgiveness you must gain hers."

Devron sat upright and looked around in stunned bewilderment. He was back in his meditation room. He touched his head, and then held out his arms to look at his clothing. Everything was as it should be. He slowly lay back and again went through *Leen-odd Nimm Bare-ehth* to clear his mind. He had no doubt that he had seen his blessed patron, the Unicorn Queen, herself. His pain from what he had done was still there, but not enough to drive him to madness. He wondered if he had actually given way to his more base passions. The Mularian or Wild Elf, princess had once told him, 'the two clans were not so different. Where they (the Wild Elves) embraced the feelings they had, the High Elves were too stoic or haughty to even admit they had feelings.' Then Cellerun went on, 'I bet when you make love to your woman, you close your eyes so you don't see what you have been missing.' Devron had been celibate in his stoic pursuit of evil; his own code of conduct wouldn't allow him that pleasure, which was ironic, as the order he belonged to, had encouraged its members to marry. The theory was they had to learn to separate different facets of their life and draw strength from everything around them.

Devron slowly ended his meditation as hunger made his stomach rumble. He stood and slowly made his way to another part of the building. He still wondered about this place. He could vaguely understand what had happened, that it was some kind of refuge, and his mind controlled things to a degree. He entered the eating room where cushions surrounded the low marble table. Devron could see one place set, so carefully as to not bump his knees, he sat. He looked up amused at the thought. He had so often smacked his knees on the table when he was young. Even now he could hear his *nah-nehth*, his mother, gently scold him for being so clumsy. Devron settled at his place inhaling deeply the delicate aroma, sighing in contentment, *wehn tee-oo-roo*, maiden cheese, or as humans called it, elven bread. His n*ah-nehth* used to make her own. She had put finely diced apples with raisins into the leavened dough, and then coated the whole wafer with honey. Outsiders never understood the name, they though that maiden cheese was made by young girls with an urn. They couldn't grasp that the cheese part of the name came from grain that grew in the ground fertilized by moldy cheese.

He looked at the two cakes as big as his outstretched hand. He felt a pang of homesickness, *nah-nehth* always looked after him, he had been born such a small baby, and he had been teased relentlessly for it. A small goblet of honey cider sat next to the plate. Devron quickly squashed any thoughts of home, or any memories of that time long ago. That was another lifetime, and lingering in the past didn't help matters now. But, for that single moment he loitered, enjoying the meal.

Devron walked through his gardens, normally there would have been a dozen servants working. He bit into the bread savoring the taste, and wondered what to do next. If he had been home he would have gone to the *bahr-ahd*, his private training tower. The elf shrugged, why not? He turned down a small path that wound its way through the lush setting. Birds with brightly colored plumage picked at the grass in search of food.

He paused before the heavy wooden door and with a quick bow, he whispered, "For the experience we are about to receive, may Nimm Bare-ehth, guide us with her blessing."

Normally another servant would be here to assist with his armor, but now he was alone. He pushed through the door and mounted the small stairs to enter a training room. He paused, and sighed in deep satisfaction, seeing his armor as it hung on the wall in its displayed state. He bowed briefly, and intoned the small blessing as he took down each piece. The breastplate, while light, provided him more protection than the heavy plate armor that the Outsiders wore. He paused, seeing the detailed scrollwork that had been etched into it. Gold filigree filled the small grooves. He closed his eyes remembering the day it had been fitted. The artisans procured the heavy metal armor needed, and poured acid in the tub that held it. The armor began to dissolve, and soon it was just melted slag. Then, they ritualistically added the milked sap from the yew tree into the bath, which neutralized the acid. Devron remembered slowly climbing into the tub, and submerging his body; the yew sap trapped the liquid metal, and bound it to the elf's body. The tub was then emptied, and artisans came to attend to the warrior as the mixture cooled and hardened. It was molded perfectly to his graceful body, and the hardening metal had to be carefully separated at his natural joints enabling the elf to retain full movement. Then, as the armor continued to cool, the suit was sent to the magical forges. The result was the equivalent of the drow adamantine or the dwarven mitheril armor, lightweight and impervious to almost all attacks, both magical and conventional.

Devron was just about to prepare for the small ceremony for the re-joining of the armor when he heard a whinny. He froze and with an unfamiliar cry of human delight, he bolted from the room, taking the small flight of stairs, three at a time. The elf dodged past the center fountain bubbling with flowing water, and darted down another path. He stopped briefly as he spied the stables, and then hurried through.

"Sabula, is it really you?"

Devron looked in dazed awe as the unicorn came trotting up to him; the snort of pleasure was genuine. The elf stroked the velvet muzzle as the animal nuzzled him.

"How can this be, you would have died over a thousand years ago?"

Devron froze as he heard a voice holler.

"Hello the house."

Devron harrumphed; another human gesture. He must re-enter the meditation trance, purge his thoughts of these disgusting lapses, he couldn't help looking quickly about in case anyone noticed.

Count Alex Richmond dan Ture, reined in his horse and sat watching the marble building he could vaguely see through the trees. He twisted around in surprise as a deer burst from the foliage and bounced off.

"From the looks of things Jenny, his mind has recovered quicker than the others have."

Jenny didn't even bother pausing in her grazing as the frogman talked to her.

He sighed irritably as the headaches started again. He pulled the black leather glove from his hand, and with a very human looking appendage he fished out the water-skin. He also took a cloth from an oilskin. He doused the fabric, and then resealed the bag. He removed his wide-brimmed hat, and using the wet cloth he wiped his head and face. As soon as the liquid seeped into the amphibian skin, the headache immediately began to dissipate. Alex looked at the webbing between his fingers, and sighing replaced his glove. He glared at the peaceful setting before him. He had worked for centuries to fix the mess. He had made a great deal of progress in restoring his old body; unfortunately some of the results weren't what he had hoped for, like the webbing between his fingers. He knew without looking, there was webbing, likewise between his toes. The majority of his body was now human except for the upper shoulders and head, given another couple of months, he might have actually have made it. He twisted slightly in the saddle looking back to where he had left Justina some hours ago; he knew they would arrive someday, he just knew it. Alex fingered the sword and wondered if he would be able to fix things this time. He did, after all have hundreds of years to practice. But his sudden confidence evaporated. He had been self-assured the last time as well, too overconfident as it turned out, and things had ended disastrously. He looked at the settlement, and wondered that after all that had happened, would he be able to murder the man … this very man he now waited to meet. Alex stared moodily at the mare as she shifted her weight while she grazed. He would have to strike when the other was unaware, otherwise the newcomer would be too good, and Alex would never be successful, and he would fail again. He spurred Jenny forward cruelly. The mare jumped.

"Sorry girl, you didn't deserve that, did you?"

Alex dismounted and let the mare's reins drag as she grazed. He looked about and was impressed with what he saw. It had taken him months to get to the stage where he could actually get living creatures to appear. He still hadn't been able to 'create' a live human to appear. He shrugged sheepishly; maybe that kind of thing should be left to God, after all. His Sanctuary had constructs working in the estate, but no live or sentient beings had appeared yet. He wondered if the newcomer had been able to do so yet, and that idea strangely irked him. He turned and watched the elf walk up from one of the outbuildings.

"Greetings, I am Count Alex Richmond dan Ture." He dropped in to an extravagant bow, and he swept off his hat.

Devron slowed and carefully approached. He glanced curiously at the ground-reined mare grazing peacefully; intrigued, he looked at the frogman. His evaluation took in his elaborate clothing and the dueling rapier on his belt.

"*Kah-bore*," the elf answered haughtily.

Alex winced inwardly, he had expected nothing less.

"Frog, Well I guess it fits."

The elf looked surprised. He hadn't thought a simple Outsider would know the Edhel.

"What do you require?" he asked.

Alex smiled, even after all these years he still sounded like a typical point-eared git. "I have appointed myself as sort of a welcome wagon. I try to visit all the new arrivals. As you have probably already figured out, the Sanctuary caters to your personal needs. You are able to manipulate the 'stuff' this little world is made of to a limited degree."

The elf stood with his arms folded, watching. Yet, as he stood there, something about the creature in front of him bothered him.

"Have we met before? I feel as if I should know you?" Devron asked hesitantly.

It wasn't so much the clothes, or the actual look of the man, but something inside. Devron had the divine gifting, to see to a limited degree, how a person was aligned to the faith. Intoning a few mystic words now, the elf could see a bright blue glow from the man; there were actually two versions of blue, one on another. Alex stood patiently waiting; he knew what the paladin would be doing. They were always trained to detect evil before a potential enemy got close enough to kill them. The elf faltered, he had seen an aura like that only once before, in another brother of the order. Devron struggled, his order never knew of another holy chapter outside Vanwa Hir.

"Have you sworn vows?" the Elf asked reluctantly.

Alex nodded. "I met a woman, and with the blessing of my church and order, I settled down to marry her."

Devron faltered, he had heard of such a man. He had led the relief force from the south that helped break the drow invasion of the Mystic Isle. It was that kingdom, he chose to attack after he had regained his strength, and he had risen as an undead. He had led a Minotaur army, devastating the country in revenge. It was there he killed the king and had taken his queen as an undead creature of his creation, and went on to try and curse the daughter.

"Michael?" Devron asked suddenly unsure.

"That man is dead; he has been now for a thousand years." Alex took a step forward. "What are we to do about this, for I know exactly who you are, and what you have done?" Alex flared angrily and lunged up in Devron's face, his hand quivering on the handle of his sword.

His own honor stopped him from killing an unarmed man. "It was bad enough to kill me, when all I wanted was to defend my home, protect my family, but you had to... to...do what you did to my wife, and my daughter." His anger got the best of him, and he drew the sword, grabbing the elf by the front of his shirt. "I should kill you here and now!" he thundered, his sword pricking Devron's chest, his hand shaking with emotion.

Devron knew no fear, as a paladin, his training overcame fear, and the creatures that radiated it. But here and now, he was suddenly afraid that he would die before he had a chance for forgiveness from Nimm Bare-ehth. He gathered his fortitude and sank to his knees, and bent forward on his arm, baring his neck for the killing blow.

"Make it swift." When Alex hesitated, Devron looked up, "If you expect me to beg, I will not." The tone was haughty.

Alex quivered and indecision stilled his hand. All the years since he came here, he wanted nothing more than to be in this position, but here and now, he knew he couldn't do it. He still had to live with himself, and since his arrival; he knew it was going to be a long time. Devron sighed in relief. He had gambled that the man was too honorable to kill a defenseless man; he had gambled ... and won.

Devron said, "Allow me this grace, I would return to Nimm Bare-ehth's benevolence, but to do that I must gain another's forgiveness."

Suddenly, with startling insight he knew Devron meant Justina.

"You ... have ... got ... to ... be ... kidding!" he gasped incredulously. "Do you think for one minute, that she will even let you close to her when she regains her memory? Do you think she will thank you for her life as a banshee, or trying to turn Justine to a vampire!" he raged. "Are you really that bloody stupid?"

20

Alex pulled himself back from the madness that threatened to claim him.

"Since coming here, I have learned to do many things, I have learned magic, and how to manipulate the stuff this place is made of, but I think I have more chance of fixing what 'you' did to me, than do, getting Justina to forgive you!"

Devron looked up derisively. "I do not recall having done anything to you personally."

Alex bent over to look him in the eye. "The day you arrived in front of your mighty army, under the 'Code of Chivalry' I approached to engage you in personal combat. If I won, you had to leave. I stood ready, and you used magic, changed me into a frog, and then used the teleport spell to send me into nothingness. I came here, where I have spent my days, waiting for you, hoping one day someone would kill you, and your body might end up here," Alex ended wearily.

Devron still on his knees; didn't know what to say. He knew all about the honor of personal combat.

"Allow me the grace of one month. If, in that time I fail, I will meet you as honor dictates."

Alex had an angry retort on his lips, about how a creature like Devron had any inkling about honor, but something stayed his tongue.

"I will give you your month. But, know this, if anything happens to Justina, in any way, I will be back, and you, in your dishonor will have to fight me."

* * *

Sanctuary Three

The hunter came plodding out of the forest, the doe draped across both shoulders. The man was close to six feet, with wide, well developed shoulders. His arms were muscular from years of hard work. The bow in his hand and the sword in the worn scabbard hinted at a man who knew how to take care of himself. The face hadn't seen a razor in days, and the dark hair was long and lank. His deep-set eyes under bushy eyebrows never stopped moving. His keen hearing already detected what his prowling gaze missed. Even his astute sense of smell worked to help him survive.

It had been four days since he had mysteriously appeared here. It didn't take long to find the well-stocked cabin. The building had been simply furnished, a nice comfortable bed with warm blankets, and a wide deep fireplace with a cooking pot hanging on a swing hook. Outside, the woodpile was well stocked, and the axe, sharp; a short distance off was the outhouse. The little cabin was everything he had ever wanted. Up to now, soldiering in the Slaver Army had left him little time of his own. Then, one night the advance scouts had captured two women, and they had been brutally beaten for the killing of two guards. He had been on watch, when strangers appeared out of nowhere, and he had been shot with an arrow. He remembered the arrow had a blue glow on it, as the magic flittered away. He stopped walking, remembering the screaming pain, then the light quickly enveloped him, and suddenly he was here, laying in the wide meadow a few short miles away from the cabin. He still didn't know what had happened, or where he was, but one thing he did know, he couldn't have been happier. Now, all he needed was a woman. He smiled to himself, and repositioned the carcass on his shoulders, and headed up the hill to where the cabin overlooked the valley.

The hunter drew a burning stick from the fireplace, then leaned back on a sturdy wooden chair, lighting the pipe he held, as he puffed furiously to start it. Then, putting the dishes from the meal of venison steak, and the fried potatoes in a bucket with water, he went outside to sit in the warm evening. He tilted the chair on its back legs, and put his booted feet up on the railing. This was the most beautiful place he had ever seen. The moon, low and big in the night sky, reflected off the lake in the valley. He inhaled deeply, sighing in contentment watching the clouds, light against the night sky drifting majestically above the pipe smoke. He gazed leisurely at the forest, nodding appreciatively as two does, and a buck glided silently into the meadow cradling the lake, highlighted by the moon. When drowsiness set in, he yawned and clumped the chair back on its own legs, stood and stretched his back heading inside.

He had just taken his boots off and set the sword belt aside, hanging it on the end of the bed, when he heard footsteps outside. The sound was soft, each carefully placed. For some reason the intruder missed the squeaky section of the porch. The hunter swiftly leapt for the end of the bed, and quietly pulled the long sword free. The door lever moved minutely, and then started to move inward. The faint grate from some forgotten stone on the floor stopped the intruder. It was a second later that a hand appeared on the door and a woman peeked carefully around the edge. The man was suddenly interested; it had been months since he even had a chance at a girl. Then, he'd had to wait in line as the men before him had their go. He settled back on the bed, warily keeping the sword close. The woman came fully into the cabin, and stood there. She was a real beauty, almost as tall as he was, her honey blond hair was long, and silky. She wore an asymmetrical leather skirt and a separate halter type garment over her well-endowed bust. She didn't say a word, but stood provocatively, one well formed, nicely defined leg was thrust forward, and from where he sat it was possible to see clear to her shapely hip. She wore nothing underneath, not the garments the women of his race wore, or the skimpy loincloth of the cat people. He settled back on the bed, and carefully laid the sword down … where he could still get to it if he needed.

The woman, still not saying a word, slowly undid the single tie holding the halter closed, moving to him. As the leather fell clear, she carefully straddled his lap, and then leaned forward, kissing him deeply; her probing tongue was everywhere. She moved with him as

23

he slid back on the bed. She briefly turned, and blew out the lantern plunging the cabin into darkness.

* * *

The horse moved slowly up the trail from the lake. Alex looked thoughtfully at the cool clear water as they passed. A longing urged him to stop, and indulge in the soothing embrace. Alex jerked upright; he had been riding slightly hunched over, like a sack of wheat. He suddenly grumped; he knew where the water urge came from. He had never been a big fan of swimming when he was young, almost drowning as a child cured those feelings. The sun was just now rising over the mountain peaks, and the whole side of the valley was still shadowed. He sighed, and shook his head in frustration, he had meant to get here yesterday, but the stop at the elf Sanctuary had taken longer than originally planned. So he had returned home, and then started early this morning to come here. The three-hour ride had left him stiff and tired. Strangely enough he now found his movements sluggish. His whole demeanor was lackadaisical and his mind slightly befuddled. He shivered in the early morning mist, and snuggled deeper into his woolen greatcoat, the elaborate stitching and design beautifully rendered. He hated the cold; he had an almost over-powering urge to sleep. Fortunately the sun was rising. He glanced up at the mountains, shuddered seeing they were covered in snow. Alex stared at the sight in dazed tribulation. Something was wrong; it had never snowed here before. But then, this new person might come from a colder climate. Alex shook his head to clear the rambling thoughts, a sure sign he was suffering from hyperthermia. He prodded the mare, and with a whinny, she plodded on.

Alex awkwardly dismounted and looked around in admiration. He could hear the steady sound of wood on wood. The frog creature quickly drew his sword, and looked carefully into the shadowed depths of the forest. The rhythmic bang, bang seemed to come from inside. He put the sword away, now pretty sure he had identified the source. But that brought more questions, how could the newcomer have been able to summon a female so soon? Either that or he had been here longer than Alex had been aware of, or someone else was here, new to the 'Stuff.'

24

The frogman walked forward to the porch, and just as he was about to set foot on the first wooden step, he hesitated suddenly embarrassed; his foot paused in midair. Unexpectedly, at a loss as what to do, he slowly stepped back. He looked at Jenny, and the nearby trees, but neither of them offered any clue as what to do. Abruptly the door swung open, and the hunter walked out. He was dressed only in his leather breeches and stockings. The woman appeared beside him, and looked at the newcomer with sudden alarm. She hastily dressed while Alex industriously studied the hunter's woolen socks. He noticed the holes that had been carefully darned. He looked up in surprised alarm as the woman fled down the steps, having to do a twisting move that would have done an acrobat proud, to get by him.

"I guess she's not interested in anyone else." The man looked enquiringly at the frog creature. "You are adequately equipped?"

Alex looked confused.

The hunter pointed at Alex's groin. "There, you can do it, can't you?" the tone was more of curiosity, rather than the bulling taunts he had seen other children get, when he was growing up." The hunter stood with his hands on his hips watching the woman, she seemed frantic to get away. "You one of them Casanovas, mister?"

Alex's stunned mind, still groped for understanding, so he merely shook his head.

"I would like to think I'm good in the sack. Well, admit it, all men do." He looked at Alex, the eyes piercing him in place. "Do you know how many times we did it last night?" Alex could only shake his head. The hunter scratched his whiskered chin. "We did it fifteen times. What was the best you ever did?"

Alex stammered, "Three, I was lucky to get that."

The hunter bent down looking at Alex. "Any man is lucky to get that, most will be right lucky to see two in one night. That woman, every time she touched me, I was ready again. There was none of the soreness, the tired back, nothing. She went like she had been made, just for sex. We did things I had only dreamed of, or fantasized about, or heard other men talk of. I don't know what you put in the water around here, but it is a little scary. But you know what the sad thing is? If she shows up again, I will be happier than a pig in shit. Well, I guess you didn't come here for that kind of talk, come on in, and I'll fix breakfast."

Alex nodded gratefully, and followed the hunter inside. The frog creature looked around in surprise; everything was tidy, well, except for the bed. But the cabin was clean, and everything was in its place. The hunter even had water heating over the fire, and a small bucket of dishes sat next to the hearthstone.

"Stackit," the hunter said reaching out for the visitor's hand.

Alex took the offered hand and shook it warmly. He was amazed that a total stranger would accept him so freely, and his hospitality was cordial, and friendly, especially considering the way Alex looked.

"Call me Alex." He turned and with a sideways twist, sent his wide brimmed hat spinning to the hook on the wall, and it bounced once and settled on the wooden peg.

"Not bad," Stackit said admiringly.

"It's funny; when there isn't much of a life, how quickly little things become important. Stackit, kind of an odd name, didn't your parents like you?" Alex joked.

The big man grinned heartily. "Not sure to be honest. I grew up in an army camp. When I was young enough to be of value, I carted supplies and the officer's gear around. They would just say 'stack it there'. So, given no proper name I kind of latched on to that one."

Stackit talked as he mixed flour and water, and then stoked up the metal oven in the corner. "Pancakes, what I remember of my ma, she made delicious pancakes." He paused and stared into nothing. "I was five when the army took me. Then ma was passed on to the next man."

"Sorry about that," Alex offered.

Stackit grinned. "Don't worry, it didn't pay to. Our whole culture was geared for feeding boys into the army. It seemed women were not counted for much. They were either on their backs, pregnant or dead. Our leaders were waging a war against the 'vile' Koldorians. They were a race of cat people who live in the land my ancestors found themselves in, as they fled the destruction of their homeland. I personally think they were all right, but you didn't voice that kind of sentiment. It made for a painful experience. Actually, now that I think about it, I have seen your picture before. I mean, not as a frog. But I recognize that get up you're wearing, but the picture was with a crown. One of the original settlers took it from the temple

26

where some woman had been entombed. Not sure why, personally I think the portrait was taken as a replacement, or a trophy of some kind, a reminder of what he had been forced to leave behind. The story goes on that whoever the man was, had been cheated, and lost the girl in the tomb.

Alex grimaced, but the hunter's back was turned and he missed seeing the look of misery pass over the frogman's face.

Alex gathered his resolve and said, "Well, I have set myself up as a sort of welcome wagon. I have learned to adapt the stuff this place is made of, so I am able to get a little information on whoever comes over." Alex looked at Stackit perplexed. "I haven't been able to get any information on you through. But anyway, each person has what we refer to as a Sanctuary. It is a place where each person lives. It caters to each individual's needs."

Stackit looked around the cabin. "I had already pretty much guessed that. Mister, are we dead? The last thing I remember was being shot with a blue glowing arrow."

Alex sighed. "To be honest, I'm not sure. From what I have found out, this is where people go who have had accidents, or make mistakes with magic. So while we probably are dead in the real world, we seem to get a second chance here."

"How long do we live, and are we able to die again?"

"As to how long you stay, I'm not sure. I have been here a thousand years. A few others have been here longer. And other than some change in my appearance I have not aged a day. But in answer to your second question, yes you can die here."

"Why have we been brought here? I mean there are other 'residence' here, right?"

Alex squirmed. "He nodded; there are bout two hundred beings here. Some have come from worlds similar to yours, and mine; some come here from planes, or worlds that are so totally different that they need special places to live, like creatures from the nine circles of hell. They are creatures of fire, or cold, or merely gaseous. These more specific beings seem to have to stay within the boundaries of their individual Sanctuaries. As to why, I don't know, yet."

Stackit place a hot round object on Alex's plate. "Sit; there is honey on the table. You'll love this." He went to sit down, "Why, yet."

27

Alex poured honey over the pancakes, and watched intrigued as the warm surface melted the sticky thick paste-like substance. He took a fork and cut into it, and put it into his mouth. Alex slowly chewed with his new teeth, he had only got them back a few weeks ago, and he found he had to be careful eating, as the frog jaw wasn't as rigid as a humans, so he found biting hard on things hurt the living shit out of him.

"This is really nice," Alex moaned in appreciation.

Stackit grinned then said, "Yet?" prodded Alex.

"Little things have started happening. Sometimes the fruit is spoilt, or one of the birds dies. It's nothing that in the real world would even rate a remark. But here, it has become disturbing."

"Like a woman who can shag all night, knows your every desire, and doesn't say a word."

Alex looked up startled. "What was that you said?"

"That woman, she squirmed, and twisted, but never made a sound. Having sex is one of the noisiest things a couple can do. They grunt, whimper, moan and make a dozen other sounds. Last night, I was the only one making noise. She didn't, not once. Mister, are there any other people living around here without one of these sanctuary things."

"Actually there are. Think of Stuff as being a wide oblong circle, with the designated Sanctuaries forming an inner ring within the larger one. Inside the inner circle, is what is referred to as No Man's Land. This area covers a few hundred miles. Some of the creatures that are created, like your deer don't recognize the borders, and they roam freely. Over the years, there has been a real mixed bag of life that lives in No Man's Land. I for one avoid it, as it is not a good place for a frog to get caught. There is a race of elves that live there. They call themselves Shadow Elves. It seems that they once lived in the Shadow Realm, and creatures there found their hiding place and attacked. As the Shadow Elves were creatures of magic, and the Shadow Plane was magic as well, when they died, they found themselves here, or more precisely, No Man's Land. They think they are cursed, and this is their hell. The one thing I can tell you is … they really like frogs. But, they are wild, and fear coming into the Sanctuaries. But if you are caught in their part of Stuff, well you are fair game as far as they are concerned."

28

"You referred to this," Stackit waved to the world outside the cabin walls, "as Stuff. Why?"

Alex looked sheepish. "Well, to be honest, I don't know. This whole 'world' is what a mage would call a mini plane. I can tell you what the magician's explanation for the creation is, but to keep it simple, I call it Stuff. I guess for no other reason than I felt it needed a name, like No Man's Land. I am sure the Shadow Elves have their own name for the area, or even for themselves."

The hunter stood. "How about a nice cup of coffee, or do you prefer something else, cocoa?"

Alex's keen hearing caught a faint buzzing sound, a quick hunger pain shot through him, and as Stackit stood, and took the dishes. Alex cast quickly around. He heard Stackit speak again.

"What?" he said absently, "Oh, yes that will be fine."

As soon as the hunter turned, Alex twisted and located the big blowfly that hovered near the scraps from last night's meal. Abruptly a long pink tongue shot out, and nabbed the fly and as the hunter returned with two steaming mugs, Alex sat back, hands folded across his stomach, looking quite smug.

* * *

Sandra

Sandra stood on the porch of the Sheriff's Office in Black Lake Colorado. She turned as the man followed her out, and shut the door firmly. Richard Danby moved towards her as she waited, reaching for her. Sandra freely took the offered hand. She kissed it lightly. Richard draped his arm over her shoulders pulling her closer.

"Are you sure you need to go?" he asked softly.

The woman nodded, her long honey blond hair bounced softly against the man's face where she leaned into him. "Unfortunately … yes, I have to be in Washington day after tomorrow. The House Arms Services Committee meets Wednesday, and I have a bit of homework to catch up on. But the Easter break is only a few months off, and I have more than enough leave owing when the current review is finished. I will take some time off, and we can go 'camping' like you were talking about earlier."

The couple stood silently on the porch; Richard had the sudden feeling that … he wasn't sure. But, her reached out and pulled her closer. He could feel the beat of her heart. Her forehead rested against his chest.

"'What's the matter? You look like you've seen a ghost," Sandra asked concerned.

Richard mentally kicked himself. "It's nothing, must be nerves left over from the murder investigation. Are you sure you don't want me to take you back to your place in the jeep? I could get one of the Thomson kids to bring Sultan over later."

Sandra weakly pushed herself back from him, she shook her head. She could feel the heat from his body. "You just want one more for the road."

Richard grinned. "Well, if you want. I guess you could twist my arm."

Sandra reached up and kissed him lightly. "You really are a dirty old man."

"Hey, not so much of the old," he said with pretended indignity. Then, he sobered. "You just make sure you're careful."

"Richard, you are a dear, but it's only a five mile ride to the cabin, it's my way of saying goodbye to such a peaceful place."

They separated as they heard the clomp, clomp of a shod horse on the asphalt road.

Sandra stepped down off the porch steps, reaching for the leather reins. "Thanks, Billy; I'll leave Sultan at the cabin. It will be Easter before I get back."

"Sure thing, Congresswoman."

Billy and his girlfriend Stacy looked after the horse and the cabin when she was away.

Sandra looped the reins back over the big black gelding's graceful head. The horse softly nickered, and nuzzled Sandra in the chest. The woman reached up for the battered brown cowboy hat hanging on the saddle horn, and smoothed the curls from the side of her face, carefully settling the hat. Richard whistled, even in her denim Levi's, the snug corduroy jacket, and her plaid snap button shirt, she still looked every bit the sensual, beautiful woman he had grown to love. Sandra lightly swung up in the saddle, and reached down taking the Winchester from Billy, slipping it into the rifle scabbard. Richard walked up, and patted the gelding's neck, then rubbed the woman's thigh gently.

Unexpectedly anxious, she said, "I will see you in a few months."

Richard impulsively reached up, and pulled her forward, gently kissing her suddenly quivering lips, her startling blue eyes full of unshed tears.

"I love you," he whispered softly.

Sandra returned the kiss. "I love you too."'

With that she reined the horse, and with a gentle kick, the gelding was moving. At the edge of town she paused briefly and turned in the saddle. Richard was where she left him. He blew a kiss, and waved to her. Sandra smiled, and then she too blew a kiss and waved.

The afternoon sky was clear, not a cloud could be seen. The air this late in the year, at this altitude was cool, and she was grateful for her jacket. Sultan moved carefully down the trail, it was heavily cluttered with fallen debris. Most of it must have come down in the storm a few days ago. She smiled, the park rangers would be upset, there was going to be a lot to clean up. Suddenly Sultan stopped dead in his tracks; his head went up, his ears twitching forward as he searched the trees for some kind of disturbance. Sandra shucked the rifle as she felt the horse quiver, and he whinnied, a short sharp noise. The woman was aware now of a buzzing sound, almost like a chain saw. Sultan fidgeted, and shifted his feet. She booted him gently, and they went forward slowly. The sound of her leveling a round into the chamber made her jump; she hadn't realized she was so keyed up. But the memory of the murdered marines, and her best friend's assault by a mentally deranged man still haunted her. She had fled screaming. Four months in therapy had helped. That was one of the reasons she had come to Black Lake. To help her shattered nerves relax.

They rounded a small bend in the trail, and Sandra stopped the horse, staring in astonishment. She could see a body lying in the brush. Slowly Sandra dismounted, and holding Sultan's reins tightly, she walked cautiously forward. Sandra stopped, she wasn't sure she wanted to go any further. Why in hell did she have to say goodbye. They would have been home in the jeep by now. Sultan jerked his head, pulling her back as they heard the howling of wolves. She shook her head, what was going on. Black Lake didn't have any wolves. She jumped as one stepped into view, straddling the body on the ground. She blanched. It was the size of a small pony. The animal snarled, and growled at them. Another stepped into view, then a third. The body weakly moved at their feet.
"Don't move." Sandra whispered urgently.

She yelped in fearful surprise, Sultan whinnying in fear as two of the wolves leapt to attack. Now, faced with the moment of judgment, Sandra almost faltered, she let loose the reins when Sultan jerked his head, pulling the leather traces from her hand. With no choice now, she either had to fight or die, and Sandra fervently wanted to live. Unexpectedly a serene calmness settled over her, and coolly she drooped to one knee; in the classic stance she favored when she was shooting on the Air Force Academy Rifle Team, she held her breath, and slowly squeezed. The sharp crack of the Winchester stopped the wolf in his tracks as the bullet slammed into his chest. She quickly worked the lever, and fired a second time. Now, the last wolf was moving and Sandra didn't even hesitate, the

32

rifle barked a third time, and the last attacking wolf went down with a high-pitched yelp.

Sandra fished three shells from her jacket pocket and reloaded the rifle before approaching the body. With the rifle still seated against her shoulder, she cautiously edged forward. Sandra kicked the closest animal, and quickly stepped back ... waiting. Sighing with relief, and suddenly light headed from the sudden release of adrenalin, she leaned over, her hand on her knee until the giddy feeling passed, the rifle still gripped tightly in the other. She made sure the remaining two wolves were dead. Sandra quickly approached the body, which she could see was a woman. Sandra knelt beside her, and swiftly looked for injuries. There was none the Congresswoman could see. The woman was about her own height, and had the same colored hair, but Sandra was unable to get a good look at her as she lay face down. She carefully propped the gun against the tree, and rolled the woman onto her back. The Congresswoman gave a squeal of astonishment, and literally jumped back a few feet, falling to sit on the ground. Sandra was looking at a face that mirrored her own. The woman was dressed in a torn cotton shift that ended just inches above her torn and dirty knees. The ragged and tattered clothing barely provided her any modesty. Her face looked puffy, and there was a swollen lump on her forehead.

Sandra Redwood sat there frantically thinking about what to do when she heard footsteps behind her. She spun around, and sighed in relief seeing Sultan picking his way to where she sat. Sandra carefully climbed to her knees, retrieving the rifle, and looked into the suddenly dark and forbidding forest. Seeing nothing she ran to the horse, which jerked his head up, the reins flying at the unexpected move. She quickly sheathed the rifle, and then spent a few minutes quieting the distressed animal. When the horse had stopped shaking, she was able to take a sugar cube from her jacket pocket; she took up the reins, and carefully led the animal around the dead wolves.

Sandra sat in the saddle propping up the woman who now sat sidesaddle in front of her. Her head lolled against Sandra's chest. She gently kicked the gelding; they were only a mile or so from the cabin. As they started moving, Sandra was once again aware of the buzzing sound. It actually seemed to be getting louder. They rounded

33

a rocky outcrop and Sandra violently pulled on the reins. Sultan whinnied in fear, and reared. Sandra had her hands full for a few seconds controlling the frightened horse, steadying her own racing heart, and keeping the unconscious woman from falling out of the saddle. It had taken Sandra long enough to get her here, she wasn't about to let the girl fall.

"Whoa boy. Easy there," her voice was soft and soothing. With one firm hand on the reins, she patted the animal's neck with the other.

They were looking at a large blue hole softly shimmering, suspended in the air across the path. The size expanded, and contracted as they watched. The buzzing sound seemed to be coming from the blue circle. She could see the trail through the light. The woman sat there puzzled, but as it didn't seem to be doing anything, Sandra slowly calmed, when she settled, Sultan responded. After a few minutes wondering what it was, and what to do, Sandra could feel the woman stir. The unknown woman's body stiffened in panic, jerking upright, smacking Sandra in the bottom of her jaw. Light exploded before her eyes, and she swayed, fighting the sickening nausea that threatened to consume her. Sandra's head spun, and her eyes filled with tears; Sultan, feeling his rider's reflexive movement shied sideways.

The passenger put her hands across her face in terror and screamed a soundless cry. Sandra was filled with an unexpected, overwhelming dread; she could feel panic surge through her body, sobbing with fear. They had to run, but her mind was too numb to do anything. Sandra whimpered, a tiny little girl sound as Sultan shifted his weight, jerked his head forward pulling the reins free. The unknown woman just held her face with her trembling hands, and silently screamed in terror. The woman started squirming, kicking wildly to get away, and in the process her flailing legs kicked the horse. The animal jumped forward … through the blue circle and then stumbled on a root, stumbled to his knees. Both women were thrown forward landing awkwardly, the horse scrambled to his feet, and trotted off a short distance. Sultan stopped and turned to look for his rider. Both women lay quietly on the grass.

Slowly the buzzing faded, and then the light dimmed, the circle shrank in on itself, and then with a small puff of light it was gone.

Sandra moaned weakly as she felt something plucking at her chest. She groaned and looked up through blurry eyes, and could see Sultan, his plucking lips working at her jacket pocket, trying to get to the sugar cubes. She slowly pushed him away and rolled to her side, gradually levering herself up. She looked around in dazed bewilderment, rubbing her forehead, and could see the woman she had rescued laying in a small heap off to the side of the path. Sandra went to stand, and suddenly grabbed blindly for Sultan to steady her swimming head. She fingered the split on her forehead, and probed the swollen knot around it. She glanced again at the woman, and unsteadily made her way to her. Sandra absentmindedly brushed the leaves and dirt from her clothing. She used her fingers as a crude comb to rid her hair of any debris. Sandra leaned against a tree, and looked sadly at the woman. It looked as if she had broken her neck hitting a fallen log. She sagged to the ground, and reached out to the woman. Abruptly Sandra stopped her hand, suddenly afraid to touch her. The last time Sandra had touched her; the Congresswoman had been filled with an all too familiar panic and terror. She whimpered as she sat on the ground, it had been the same feeling she had experienced in Antarctica, when she had fled after the four marines had been brutally killed. She looked at the dead woman and using the trees to help her stand, couldn't get away from the body fast enough.

Sandra pushed Sultan as hard as she dared; it had only been a mile further on to get to her house. But, in the back of her mind she heard the niggling phrase she had remembered from an old movie, 'You're not in Kansas anymore.' The rider paused at a small stream, and slid from her horse. She was pretty sure now something was wrong. They had been riding for hours, and had easily covered five miles. She walked to the edge of the water and squatted down, and using her cowboy hat dipped out the liquid, and in an impulse poured it over her head, she squealed as the cold water seeped down her back and soaked her shirt front. Sandra looked around hopefully; nope she was still here. She settled back on a small rock and gazed

35

skyward. She sat so long her neck hurt. Not once did she see the elusive jet trail of a highflying aircraft. She sobbed once, and the pity party that had been rapidly approaching began to take hold.

Suddenly, Sultan snorted angrily. She looked up to see what looked to be a dozen flying creatures, each the size of a basketball. They swarmed about the gelding, and she could see that as some landed on his back they were drawing blood. The horse bucked, and thrashed around trying to dislodge them. She cried out with righteous indignation, and grabbing a nearby broken branch ran forward, screaming. Sandra used the limb like a baseball bat and swung hard. She missed the first but connected solidly with the second. The body was crushed, and blood splattered everywhere. These creatures were an upsized version of mosquitoes like they had back home. The woman's spirits faltered when she saw more of the big bugs winging their way from one of the bigger trees. Some of them attacked her, and she found herself hard pressed to defend both her and the horse. Suddenly, she let out a startled yelp as what looked to be a miniature winged horse, far smaller than the bugs swooped down, from seemingly nowhere, and attacked the blood-sucking beasties. There were a dozen of the tiny horses, and Sandra took the chance to fight her way to Sultan. The diminutive pegasus' whirled and crashed into their prey. Sandra looked on in surprise as one of the little horses took a bite from the mosquitoes; its sharp teeth viciously tore into the soft vulnerable body of the insect. Some of the pegasus seemed to cling onto their prey, and literally eat them as they hovered, their wings whirling rapidly. The woman waded into the creek, and grabbed her cowboy hat, and the reins then, splashed quickly to the other side leading Sultan. She looked back as one of the winged horses was dragged into the water with three of the bloodsuckers clutching it. Sandra hovered, caught between fight and flight as her blood pumped hotly through her body.

"Oh hell!" she exclaimed with exasperation, and ran back into the river with big bounding steps.

She smacked one of the bugs, splattering blood all over the horse, and then the trio splashed into the river. Sandra stomped down with a big splash, and caught one under her boot pushing it down crushing it against the bottom; she gave her foot a twist, driving the heel deep into the sand. She reached into the water, and grabbed the diminutive feathered wing, and pulled it to the surface. The other bug still clung tenaciously to the animal, and Sandra grabbed it by the neck and twisted viciously. The little horse hung dangling from her hand; Sandra quickly gathered it up, and cradled it protectively in her arms, raced back to where Sultan waited. She looked back quickly, and seeing the fight still in progress, scooped up Sultan's reins and ran, leading him from the fight.

* * *

The Awakening

Justina paused at the small guardroom; the four soldiers there stood trembling in abject terror. She hovered a few inches off the ground, her dainty hands held demurely in front of her at waist height.

"How did you get out of the cell?" the tall guard yelped in frightened confusion, then more alarmed, he drew his long sword, standing there indecisively. Justina opened her mouth ... and screamed.

The woman pulled her sheets to her chin, gripped in shaking hands; her head tossed from side to side muttering in her delirium. Both her legs, still covered by the ravaged quilt moved with a life of their own. *The woman, screamed, and the four men in the guardroom died, their blood splattering everywhere. Moments later the she found herself in a dark, ancient building, the bricks and mortar crumbling, moss and slime coating the walls. A hazy gray mist seemed to cling to everything and everyone.*

A tall beautiful woman, looking so much like a younger mirror image of the older woman, she could only be her daughter, stared at Justina. Tears welled in her lovely eyes.

"Mother?" was all the younger woman could say. She began to cry.

"Child, you must kill me. Quickly before Devron crushes my will once more."

"I can't hurt you, ever!" she sobbed, her heart breaking.

The Banshee lunged at her. "Kill me now!"

The woman in the bed thrashed about. Her cries and pitiful mewing sounds were heartbreaking. Justina, suddenly found herself on the bedroom floor, eyes wide open, her mind still caught up in the nightmare, scooted backwards involuntarily. *She felt a discarded object digging into her; without thinking, she grabbed the knife, staring at the object uncomprehendingly. Instinctively, she pulled the knife from the leather sheath.*

"Justine, kill me," pleaded Justina.

"No!" her daughter's voice was breaking.

Justina sobbed in her sleep, her face a mask of despair. Her mouth moved soundlessly as the drama unfolded, and she was powerless to stop it; she knew instinctively that this was going to end traumatically.

The daughter awkwardly stood to run; the lich looking for any other intruder caught her movement and fixed his baleful glare on her. A woman, Justina knew to be Cassandra, lay slumped at his feet. So, Justine turned back to her mother. The Banshee could see Devron gathering his will again. Without warning, Justina lunged at her daughter. The Banshee tightly caught Justine's elbow, cruelly forcing the arm level, the knife pointing at herself. Justine's eyes widened with sick certainty. Justina felt heartsick, knowing this was the only way for her daughter to survive. Her pained expression swiftly changed; her face serene, filled with her undying love for her daughter. She pulled herself along the sharp blade, piercing her body just under her breast, until she could hold the weeping young woman tenderly, stroking the shoulders that were shaking with sobs. For the few seconds left to her, Justina held her daughter, the very first time in eons, and looked into Justine's sad face.

"I love you. Tell the others, I never wanted to hurt anyone."

Justina jerked awake, gasping with deep gulping breaths, her heart pounding painfully in her chest. She had subconsciously found her spare pillow, and was cradling it to her body; her slim frame was racked by huge sobs, her laments of desolation coming from deep inside. Tears streamed freely down her face, and she howled at the futility of the unfairness of it all. Slumped in bed, the dream world, her memories, reality, everything, was being superimposed on top of each other; she didn't know what was real.

She clenched her eyes shut hearing herself scream, *suddenly Justina could see the writhing vines and then felt the excruciating pain as they stabbed deep, penetrating her body.* The woman fell sideways, curled into a fetal position and tightly clamped her hands to her head, covering her ears, trying to shut out the sound of her own agonized cries. Justina shrieked in agony and hid her face in the crumpled sheets; *she saw her body, already dying falling back against the wall and slowly sliding to the floor.* Justina pulled the covers tightly over her head, *as Justine frantically crawled towards her.* She cringed and tried to bury herself deeper in the bed, then with a stomach churning crash she violently fell to the carpeted floor. Hysterically, she crawled under the four-poster bed, *trying to hide as tentacles swarmed all over her, some of them driving deep into her body. Justina collapsed as a vine stabbed up under the base of the throat.* Her head whirled in blackness and then mercifully she felt the darkness claim her.

* * *

Alex slowly followed the graveled drive, and reined in at the base of the stairs. He nodded at the changes he could see that were evident since his last visit. Justina was certainly settling in better than he believed possible. She had only been here two days. Alex sighed, and leant on the saddle horn as memories of the Summer Palace crowded in on him. They had spent the summer 'here' and it was here she had told him she was pregnant. They spent hours sitting in the swing in the garden … making plans. For the first time in years there was peace, the kingdom thrived and grew. Their youngest daughter Juliet was with Colonel Geoffrey checking the security of the artifact.

Alex sighed sadly; it had been the day after returning from the palace that the Minotaur Army had attacked. Devron had ridden triumphantly into the defeated capital. The war had been only lasted three days, and they had lost close to twenty thousand of their finest. Alex shook his head sadly; it was all such a waste. He tipped his hat from his head, and using the sleeve of his velvet tunic, wiped away the tears. He never even knew what had happened to the baby. Suddenly he jerked upright in his saddle as a scream rent the still morning.

"Bloody hell!" he exclaimed, and leapt from the saddle and barged though the front door, that suddenly was ajar, and thundered up the stairs.

"Justina! Justina! Where are you?" he thundered.

He paused for a second, and could hear sobbing from her room. Giving no thought to decorum, he bolted through the partly open door. Her bed was a shambles and he could barely make out the bare foot where it protruded from under the bed.

"Oh, dear God."

He dropped to his hands and knees, and gently called her name.

* * *

Stackit and Sandra

Sandra finished buttoning up the sheepskin jacket, and fingered the drying clothing she had staked out near the small fire. The miniature pegasus was with Sultan. She picked up the canteen, fishing a small towel from her saddlebag, and walked to where Sultan grazed. She stopped in surprise as she saw the two horses together. The gelding was eating contently while the diminutive winged equine sat on his hindquarters licking the wounds the flying bugs had caused. As she had fled the stream crossing, she had seen some pretty nasty lesion on his back. She was worried about him. But then she sighed; a lot of things scared and worried her lately. Sandra walked up softly to the animals so as not to disturb them. The torn and bloody flesh was totally healed where the diminutive horse had been licking the wound. The tiny head looked at the woman and she could almost swear the little creature was trying to convey something to her. She rubbed Sultan's back in wonder. Then, she stroked the graceful neck of the pegasus. The horse stretched his head higher exposing more area to scratch. Sandra giggled; she used to have a cat that did that very thing. She lingered for what seemed an eon, but was really only minutes. She patted Sultan's neck, and the gelding nickered, gently nosing her chest. Sandra smiled and dug a sugar cube from her pocket, and then kissed the forehead as his nibbling lips found the treat in the palm of her hand.

Sandra settled back against the rock, and laid the rifle across her lap. The hard unyielding metallic object comforted her immensely. She reached into the saddlebag, and found two small boxes of shells, each box held fifty rounds. There weren't a lot of them, and she had no idea how long she was going to be here. Grimly she put them back into the bag. She picked up the small can of spaghetti from off the fire, and leaned back against a convenient log as she ate the hot food. Sandra grimaced, she didn't like the stuff much, but the cans were easy to carry, and didn't spoil and they could take a lot of damage before they were unusable. She looked at the can, there were only a few more. Soon she would have to forage off the land. That in itself wasn't a problem. She had hunted with her dad, and later Richard often enough, but it was always comforting to have them around.

Sandra dozed in the warm afternoon sun. She had thought a lot about what to do and where to go. Then she thought of the dead woman, why did she look so much like her, they could have been sisters. She remembered that Richard had said something about a hidden lab near Black Lake. They were supposed to have been doing research in cloning. That must be it, somehow they had gotten hold of her DNA, and the newly developed woman had somehow escaped. That would explain her sudden terror, and why she couldn't talk. Sandra looked at the flying horse as it wheeled about Sultan. She sighed and her shoulders sagged. No matter how hard she tried, she couldn't convince herself they were still in Colorado. Once she admitted that single fact, that she had been so strongly trying to deny ever since the fight with the wolves, Sandra could feel a new strength slowly seep through her, and for the first time in a long, long time she was no longer afraid. She would go back, have a look for the blue hole in the air, and bury the poor woman. She settled back, more relaxed now that she had a plan, and watched the two animals frolic in the afternoon sun.

* * *

The hunter paused and with his hand shielding his eyes, glanced at the sun. It would be dark in an hour or so. He stood on a small hill, and surveyed the valley below. He was looking at the lake he had seen from the house last night, but this time from the other side of the valley. The woman has shown up again, and they had been at it all night. When she left, Stackit had followed her. Either the woman was aware she was being followed, or ridiculously lucky. In the end he lost her, and it was far too late to get back to the cabin before night. But he really didn't mind, he was used to sleeping out under the stars. They were in a way, more home to him than walls and a roof. Now, that the sun was setting for the third night, he began to look around for a place to camp. He wondered about the blond woman, the total lack of sound and her wanton endless passion was unnerving. He actually hoped she wouldn't be able to find him

43

out here. He cast one last quick look around, and then, a smudge over a small part of the forest caught his eye. It could be anyone, but in this land, anyone was not taken lightly. Still, if it was the woman he might still be able to find out something. He resettled his pack and headed off in the direction.

The sun was an hour set when Stackit found the camp. He crept silently forward. Even the night animals and many of the chirping insects were unaware of his passing. He could vaguely make out the light of a small fire. He worked his way closer and now stopped and stared in surprise, it was the blond woman. In spite of himself his body betrayed him as he watched the woman moving about the camp. She had traded the hide skirt and halter for some kind of blue breeches, and a leather jacket with some kind of fur lining; from here it looked to be sheep. Strangely, actually finding the woman frightened him. He sank to the ground behind a tree and fought to steady his racing heart and quickened breathing. Why should he fear her, after all it had been only sex? The best he had ever had, wanted or even dreamed of. Maybe that was the frightening aspect of it, she seemed to know his every desire, she knew what he was thinking, and she seemed to be able to get into his mind. Stackit drew the bow from over his shoulders, and silently notched an arrow. This would end tonight he thought. He crept closer a few feet, and found a clear unobtrusive line of sight. He drew back the long bow, and carefully sighted down the arrow. The woman turned and Stackit almost faltered seeing the press her breasts made in her shirt through the open coat. He followed her as she stood, and walked to the black horse. The animal nuzzled her, and she laughed lightly and reached into a pocket.

"There will not be many more of these left." Her voice was light and clear, her accent enchanting.

He pulled the string back to his ear, and followed her as she returned to the fire. Suddenly, it dawned on his confused mind, the woman had spoken. Unexpectedly unsure, he carefully let the string back carefully, and removed the arrow. He could hear the woman talk to herself as she busied about the fire.

He sighed in relief, it wasn't the same woman, but hard on the heels was the knowledge that he had almost killed the wrong person.

Sandra looked into the darkened night, the trees could be hiding any one of a hundred threats, and she would never know. She shrugged almost philosophically; she couldn't go for only God knows how long without any sleep. She would have to trust that the horses would wake her if anything happened. She settled under the blanket, lying back against the soft lining of the upturned saddle, the rifle close by under the blanket. After a few short moments Sandra became aware that the noises normally heard at night were suddenly gone. She looked to Sultan, he was grazing contently but the miniature pegasus was standing on a small log looking into the night. Suddenly the little horse looked at Sandra, and gave a little shrill. Sandra didn't move, she lay carefully on her side, surreptitiously edging the Winchester across her lap, and as quietly as she could levered a round into the chamber. Now, Sultan was looking off in the dark, and he gave a whinny.

Seconds later she could hear. "Hello the camp."

Sandra stirred and sat slowly.

"Hello the camp, mind if I come in?"

"Come ahead, but keep your hands where I can see them." Sandra quickly finished levering the shell into the chamber trusting her voice covered the distinct click clack of the metal.

Sandra stared in stunned confusion at the man who walked into the camp. The hunter was close to six feet tall, his rugged worn clothing, while well traveled in, were carefully mended. Sandra moaned a little, and felt her face flush as the blood surged to her head. Thin the stranger's hair out, trim up the eye brows, and add a few pounds, then dress him in a khaki uniform, and Richard Danby could be standing in front of her.

Sandra stumbled clear of the blanket, the rifle swung up sharply, her voice dropped to below zero.

"Who the hell are you, and what is this place?"

Before anyone could one could say another word the silence was shattered by crashing of dried wood, and pounding of metal on metal. Sandra and Stackit looked around as a tall, lithe woman dressed in leather body armor, a wide leather metal studded skirt reaching mid-thigh, and her shapely legs encased in leather greaves raced toward them. Her long blond hair was tied back in a ponytail. The long sword and shield she carried were clearly visible as she ran into the camp. Sultan shied away and the pegasus darted for the protection of the trees. Sandra's poor mind rebelled as she looked at the second mirror image of herself she had seen that day. Stackit on the other hand looked confused. This was not the seductively wanton woman who had spent the last two nights with him. The stranger stumbled to a stop, and looked at Sandra in shocked bewilderment. Her mouth moved in screams and rants, but she uttered no sound. The total absence of noise only added to her hostile appearance.

Sandra recovered first, and fired a quick shot from the hip. The sharp crack of the rife was dramatic as it was unexpected. Stackit yelped, and dived for cover. The woman's mouth froze open, and she fell to the ground when the bullet smacked into the metal shield. She groaned, dropping it with a metallic clunk hitting a stone on the ground. Sandra could see an angry red welt and a rapidly swelling bruise on her arm where the bullet had hit the metal with her arm in the straps. She glared at the Congresswoman, and gingerly holding her injured arm, darted off into the night.

Sandra gazed at the retreating woman in stunned disbelief, and sank to the log she had been sitting on, absent-mindedly digging into the sheepskin coat's pocket, and retrieved a shell, automatically feeding it into the magazine. Stackit climbed to his knees and looked at the dark forest with the same flabbergasted expression the woman wore. What he had noticed was that she had a mole over her right breast, which he could see as a result of the V-neck in her armor. That single blemish scared him more than he liked to admit.

"That's the second time I've seen that woman. The first time she screwed me silly, the next time she tries to kill me."

His voice jerked Sandra out of her musing.

"What did you say?" she asked confused.

"Do you have a mole as well?" he asked ignoring her question.

Sandra involuntarily covered her breasts with her crossed arms.

Stackit saw the movement. "So you do?"

She glared at him. "That is none of your damn business!" Sandra took a deep breath. "What did you say about that woman?"

"I've seen her before. Only she wasn't dressed as she was this time, and then we had amazing sex all night."

"With that woman?" she asked dubiously pointing into the night in the direction the intruder had fled.

"If not her, then her exact twin. Do you know the woman I slept with, knew every fantasy or thought I ever had? Every time she touched me I was ready. I managed fifteen times the first night and twelve last night. And do you know the creepiest part?"

Sandra shook her head slowly.

"Never once did she make a sound. You probably know how noisy sex is, but she never uttered a sound."

Sandra stared off into the dark again. "Just like tonight."

Stackit nodded.

She stirred uncomfortably. "I have to confess, I saw another woman that looked just like her earlier this morning. She was dressed in a torn shift, and when I found her she was out cold. Then when we were riding she woke, and after grabbing me I felt such a surge of terror and panic I could hardly breathe. She screamed and screamed in fear, but never once making a sound. Her mouth moved and her face mirrored her panic."

Stackit gazed at her in fascination. "Where is she?"

Sandra pushed her hair back, and shook her head sadly. "There was some kind of hole in the air, and when we saw it she woke, and the woman began flailing round, she kicked Sultan and he jumped through the hole. He stumbled, and fell throwing us. I woke later to find she had died in the fall, her neck broken." Sandra sat looking at him, and was again struck by how much he looked like Richard. "What's your name?"

"Stackit." He laughed lightly seeing her amused look. "I was raised in an army camp, I had no given name, and the officers used me to cart supplies, and then they simply said 'Stack it there'. So the name kind of stuck." He grinned roguishly.

Sandra laughed. "You sound a lot like someone I know from home."

Stackit asked, "I take it the other woman looked the same?" she nodded grimly. "Why do all they look like you?"

47

"I wish I knew," she fervently answered.

"They all seem to be modeled on the same person …you. But they each have a single personality, and they can't speak. If I didn't know better I would say they were never born. It is like they were made, each to do a certain thing," Stackit summed up appraisingly.

Sandra sat back reflecting. "It would seem Pandora's Box has been opened, I wonder what other surprises there are out there."

* * *

Attack

Devron followed the small ridge riding at an easy pace. The unicorn seemed to have incredible endurance and when he paused on the small hilltop to look over the valley below, the animal wasn't even breathing hard. The rider patted the mount affectionately, or as close to it as a High Elf could manage. The white hide was only slightly moist from the warm morning; a normal mount would be well lathered by now. The paladin wore his crafted, snug fitting armor with ease. Sabula wore a breastplate beautifully embossed, an elegantly designed fitted strip down the unicorn's forehead, with little lips to protect the eyes. The tack and saddle was rich in its making and it too showed elaborate care in design and manufacture. He rode tall in the saddle and his arrogant look missed nothing. He sat carefully surveying the land as if it was his own.

He slowly dismounted and knelt. "Blessed Nimm Bare-ehth, guide me as I leave the protected security your bountiful goodness has set aside for me. Protect me as I venture forth into a wild and unknown world."

He drew forth a shining amulet of gold and silver. The etching and wording in elaborate Elvish and the filigree, platinum filled, the onyx scales of balance delicately made. He reverently kissed the object and solemnly replaced his holy symbol back around his neck. He lingered, feeling the power surge through his body. He had missed the comforting feeling of peace that the symbol radiated.

Devron stood and reached for the stirrup when he heard the sounds of yelling and screaming from below. He walked carefully to the unicorn's head and stood quietly watching. He could see a rider break the trees, the horse pounding hard for the other side. He looked behind the rider and saw five strangers on smaller ponies burst into the clearing pursuing the first. Devron could see the first was armored and riding a handsome animal, but the attackers were only lightly garbed, if at all and their smaller mounts were already closing the distance. Devron hurriedly mounted and as he spurred forward he could see the first horse falter. The rider pulled the mount to a stiff legged stop and hurriedly slid from the saddle and drawing a sword, turned to face the pursuers.

49

Devron thundered off the hill and charged down into combat. He drew his own long sword from a scabbard on the side of the horse and giving his own battle cry swept headlong into the conflict. The armored unicorn slammed into the smaller ponies and bowled one, the man shrieked in terror as the animal folded, crashing to the ground trapping the rider. Devron's sword quickly silenced the screams. The paladin sprang from his saddle and waded into the fray. He battled closer to the besieged fighter, who now he could see was a beautiful woman, her long blond hair loose about her plain heavy armor. Her arm chopped and stabbed with a regular rhythmic motion that spoke of hundreds of hours of experience. Her weapon deftly caught an attacker under the chin and with a gurgling gasp he slumped to the ground. However, the fallen man grimly clutched her weapon, the sharp blade slicing his hands, severed fingers dropped to the ground. Devron turned quickly hearing the thundering hooves and spun to see six more of the savage men pour into the clearing.

"For Nimm Bare-ehth!" he yelled and charged.

* * *

Stackit and Sandra walked along the trail. The hunter had stayed in the camp in the clearing that night. He was tremendously relieved when the woman that had visited his cabin the first two nights had not appeared. He slept peacefully and contentedly. Now they walked shoulder to shoulder, Sandra leading Sultan, the miniature pegasus sitting on the gelding's back. Sandra found she was watching Stackit's profile and couldn't help but compare him to Richard. She felt butterflies in her stomach and last night as he slept she had pictured them both together. She had turned away ashamed. She knew Richard wasn't here and the man who walked beside her was a total stranger. She had no idea where to go, so Stackit was taking her to the sanctuary of the woman Alex had talked about. The only problem was the hunter had no real idea where she was, so they were backtracking Alex's horse. The trail would lead either to Alex or this woman he was enamored with.

"It's getting time to stop for lunch. My stomach feels like my throat has been cut."

Sandra stared at him; Richard used that same stupid joke all the time.

50

She could hear something, and she shushed Stackit. "Can you hear something?"

The hunter listened intently. "Sounds like someone is being attacked."

With that he was off and running, Sandra following quickly pulling Sultan along at a run.

* * *

The fight was not going Devron's way. He saw the woman slump to the ground, holding her side. One of the savage's weapons had sliced deep, penetrating her armor easily. Even now she struggled to defend herself as two attackers pushed in on her. Devron swung harder, his breathing coming in gasps as he tried to fight his way to her side. But more of the emaciated barbarians seemed to come from nowhere and he found he was seriously in danger of getting overwhelmed. There were almost thirty of them now. They must have been looking for her all over this valley and the sounds of combat had drawn the rest here. Devron grunted as he saw another blade plunge deep into her body. The paladin stumbled and three attackers swarmed over him. He erupted with a mighty yell throwing them to the ground, the blood from a cut above his eyes flowed tackily into his eyes.

"Blessed Nimm Bare-ehth, I ask for your forgiveness, let me back into your grace, even though I have failed in your assigned task!" his cry rang forth.

Devon stared in bewilderment as one of the savages plummeted at his feet, an arrow protruding from his back. A resounding snap like crash sounded and another man dropped to the ground as if he had been pole axed. Two more attackers were down, arrows in their bodies and three more were slain from the thundering noise. The screaming barbarians stopped and they all stared en masse in the direction of the trees. Another crash and the man in front of the group collapsed as his head exploded. Suddenly the savages were petrified; scrambling over each other and fleeing panic stricken in the opposite direction.

Devron hurried back to the stricken woman. She leaned feebly against a log, blood dribbling from her mouth. When she gasped in pain, blood sprayed from her nose as well. He heard the sound of thudding feet and quickly turned fearing another attack. He looked warily as the man and woman hurried forward. Sandra stopped seeing the injured woman. Stackit paused on the edge of the combat area then, he too came closer. The armored woman looked up and seeing Sandra reached out her hand. Sandra looked to the other two men for guidance and then reached for the bloodied, shaking hand.

"I found you. The Creator said you would be here soon." The woman's voice was low and Sandra had to lean forward to hear the whispered words.

The congresswoman felt a bit nauseous seeing her own blood smeared, pain wracked mirror image looking at her.

"She can talk." Stackit said incredulously.

"I...forced myself... to learn. The Creator said...I was different." She gasped and Sandra sank beside her and held tightly to the quivering hand. "The others...bad." She fumbled with a bag at her side and tried to open the drawstring. Sandra helped and the wounded woman nodded gratefully. Sandra pulled a letter out, a bit crumpled, and the name on the outside was smudged. But she had no trouble reading 'Congresswoman Sandra Redwood', to make matters even more disturbing, it was written in her own handwriting.

"Creator said... you have to be... the one to destroy the bad ones. Now... you must do like...wise to me." Her breathing was labored.

Devron moved forward and looked at her wounds. The metal armor was paper thin, making it easy to penetrate. The paladin looked confused.

"Only a human would make such armor," his tone was condescending.

"I'm sorry...but the Creator didn't know... how to do the real thing...so she...did the best she could."

"I can't kill you, I can't kill the others!" Sandra whispered harshly.

"You...must or...every...thing will be lost. For me, it is simple. Just wish me away."

They all gaped and Sandra had tears flood into her eyes.

"We can get you to a doctor. There must be one close." Sandra sniffed, her voice quivering.

The woman lunged forward, her bloody hand grasping Sandra's coat front, unintentionally jerking her forward. Sandra squealed in surprise.

"You don't get it do you? In order for the madness to be cured and this place made safe, all must die." She slumped back closing her eyes wearily, totally drained, the outburst burning out the last thread of strength she had.

Sandra knelt beside the woman; her long blond hair blowing across her exhausted face stuck to her skin in spots by the crimson stains. Sandra carefully moved it away and tucked it behind her ear. The congresswoman nodded reluctantly and the inured woman smiled gratefully. Sandra grasped the woman's hands in both of hers and she in turn weakly clasped Sandra's gloved hand. Sandra bent her head and furrowed her brow. The other Sandra gradually relaxed, and a smile spread across her face. Then in front of three bewildered people, she shimmered and collapsed in on herself. The armor flaked and lost shape falling inward, then both woman and the metal armor turned dusty, and soon the wind had scattered everything. Sandra dully looked at her arm where the bloody hand had clutched hold of her; even that mess was flaking away, dissolving.

"She's gone completely. It's like she never existed," Stackit said wonderingly.

Sandra stood and dried her eyes. "Maybe that's just it. Maybe she never was meant to be.

* * *

The Letter

The trio moved a few short miles when they halted for the noon meal. Stackit had retrieved the dead woman's horse and was now able to keep up with the other two. Devron rode ahead and deemed it unnecessary to communicate with the two humans. Stackit built a small fire and quickly made a grill of freshly cut green willows and cooked some of the venison he had brought with him.

Sandra moved a short distance and sank down leaning against a log. Sultan and the other two mounts grazed peacefully a short ways off. The little winged pegasus glided over and settled down next to Sandra. The animal stretched out his neck and Sandra automatically reached out and scratched the exposed offering. She looked at the writing on the envelope. Parts looked to be a bit shaky, while the rest was firm and complete. She looked at the white envelope and turned it over seeing a few smudges there. Sandra looked at the two men. Stackit knelt over the smokeless fire and poked at the meat with his knife. Devron sat on a small rock about ten feet away, his eyes quartering the neighboring trees and rocks. The terrain was getting rougher as they were moving into the higher mountain range.

Sandra shrugged and using her fingernail, sliced the letter open.

'Sandra, I know at this stage you are very confused, and if anything like I was, scared of everything that moves. I write this in some of my more lucid moments and I ask you to indulge me if I wander a little. I am reluctant to tell you too much for fear it might affect future events. You have probably run into images of my splintered and fractured personality.' Sandra frowned at that bit and re-read it carefully, she noticed that the writing here was different. Sandra had a good idea who wrote this, and was reasonably sure parts had been written over a varied time frame. 'At a later date which I don't think would help to tell you, earth will be hit with a massive meteor. The different countries each made preparations for the survival of their way of life. The United States built massive bunkers underground. These they stocked with literature and seeds of all kinds as well as the necessary farming equipment, fuel for both

54

flying and surface vehicles. Thousands of books on medical and surgical knowledge were carefully put away. There were also five cryogenic bunkers with ten thousand people each. I was put in one such bunker, having achieved a reasonably high level in the government, even though I didn't deserve the privilege. The incident in Antarctica had been too much for me, and in the end I never really recovered, even after the time in Black Lake. It is with that knowledge that I was able to get Hope to open the gate on the trail you would be taking home that night. However there was a breakdown in the bunker I was assigned to, and it was fifteen thousand years after the disaster that our people began to wake. Few of our instruments were still working so it was almost impossible to determine if any of the other bunkers had survived. We begin to explore our new world and found it filled with savage and often changed or mutated people and animals. Dr. Silverman our genetic biologist seemed to think a lot of what we found was a result of hundreds of years of exposure to different types and levels of radiation and other effects left over from the collision. Not really sane to start with, my anxiety and fear became overpowering. Then one day there was an explosion deep in one of the fuel storage areas and I found myself alone in this land, soon the rest of my sanity shattered. For some reason this area I suddenly found myself in seemed to be controlled by my mind and soon other people and began to arrive. One such barbaric group called themselves the Shadow Elves and I lived with them for uncounted years. I became the mad god to them and one night for reasons I can never explain I ran off in the night. The Elves thinking their god had deserted them began to search me out, with violent intentions. I hid in my sanctuary for years and then one day I began to find women who looked like me starting to appear. The bad ones; Lust, Anger, Greed, Fear and Deceit began to appear; Hope and Bravery sided with me when the others left. The last two seemed to be more intelligent than the others so I had hopes that they might find a cure for the sickness of some kind I have developed. I fear that I won't survive. Who knows what will happen to 'my little world' if I die and my mind cannot sustain this place. I have 'seen' in a 'vision' that you must destroy these facets of my troubled mind. I know what you are thinking, that I am truly mad, you wonder if I'm not in fact hallucinating. Well to be honest, I don't know for sure about anything. It is something I think

I feel strongly about and Bravery agrees enough to seek you out to get you to come and help me. My home is in the Danby Mountains. Please, Sandra I need your help, when this is finished I am reasonably certain Hope will be able to send you home.' The letter was simply signed SR.

Sandra sat looking at the letter in her hand. She re-read it twice thinking about it, tapping the paper sheets against her teeth. Then the weird thought wandered through her mind, her high school and college teachers wouldn't have been too happy about the way the letter was written. Stackit walked up and handed Sandra her meal, folded in a large leaf.

"Mean anything?"

She looked at him. "Let me think about it for a bit and then we can compare notes."

Stackit wasn't sure what she meant, but he simply nodded and sank down besides her eating his own food.

* * *

Alex carefully climbed the stairs, a silver tray carried in his hands. He paused and gently knocked on Justine's bedroom door.

"Come in." the sound was so muffled Alex could hardly understand what she said.

Using his elbow he pushed down on the lever and slowly nudged the door open with his booted foot.

Justina lay in bed, on her side. The wadded handkerchief clutched tightly in her hands. She looked up and smiled wanly. Alex walked forward and carefully placed the tray on the bedside table.

"You feeling better?" Alex asked, concerned.

He had been quite disturbed when he found her under the bed, beside herself with hysteria. He had tried to calm her down, but in the end he had to grab her ankles and pull hard. Once in bed, wrapped in the warm bedding, Justina started calming down. As she lay there still greatly distressed, Alex had rubbed her shoulders and back. She used to love that and they would spend a long time together, him stroking her back. Justina quickly calmed till she only uttered the occasional long whimper.

"Made you a pot of tea, just the way you like it Dear Heart."

Alex paused, the small silver teapot in the air. He darted a look at the woman. She leaned forward and took the cup, and sipped gently. It 'was' made the way she liked, tasting of a hint of honey and lemon.

She closed her eyes and sighed, her voice hoarse. "I haven't heard that phrase in years, and your tea is fantastic." A little sob escaped. "My husband used to make me the same type of cup and even called me by the same nick name."

Alex grimaced and darted her a sideways look. Justina just happened to be looking in his direction and wondered at his reaction. She pushed herself up straighter looking at him quizzically. The frog creature grimaced and quickly stood, he needed to break her train of thought.

"I have some herbs in my Sanctuary which I think might help you sleep better." Alex hurried on.

Justina looked at him in puzzled confusion. She barely nodded. Her heart lurched, sinking, thinking of him leaving. Things

57

didn't seem quite so bad when he was around. She sank back into the covers; both hands wrapped around her warm cup, he reminded her so much of Michael. She felt the familiar fervent burning in her body, Michael had been an exciting lover and he wasn't afraid to experiment, of taking them to exotic places, which she had eagerly followed. She didn't love her husband when they married but she quickly grew to love him deeply.

"Will you be alright for a few hours?"

"Yes, I suppose. You won't be long?" she asked as panic hovered near, there was a slight catch in her voice.

"I'll hurry; it should only take me about three hours."

Justina nodded and sank back down in bed and pulled the blanket up to her chin, her lower lip quivering as Alex left.

Justina woke abruptly, startled. She swiftly looked around and settled back, a silly grin on her face. She darted another quick glance about in embarrassment, smiling weakly thinking how stupid it was to look for someone when there was no one around. In her dream she was with Michael and they had just finished the most amazing morning. She stirred as she could hear a faint noise. She slowly surfaced, and stretched, realizing she had dropped back off. For the first time in ages she smiled. She had dreamed of the night the baby had been conceived during the last month they had been in the Winter Palace. She cocked her head toward the door hearing a sound from downstairs. Happily she sprang from bed, it must be Michael. She reached for her gown and slipped it on. Her heart sang with joy and she rubbed her tummy affectionately and a happy tune sprang from her lips. She grinned in embarrassment; she always had the urge to sing when she was happy. The door swung open to bang jarring on the wall and reality crashed in on her. Sobering clarity swamped her, Michael was dead, killed trying to defend her and Justine, she had lost the baby and now, from the looks of the woman before her, she was being robbed.

The woman who stood before Justina was tall, busty, if slightly on the lean side. She was dressed in a black leather breeches and a dark leather sleeveless tunic. A short sword was worn comfortably at her shapely hips. The woman's long blond hair was tied up in a ponytail. She dropped the bag she carried to the floor with a metallic crash. Justina cringed and looked hastily about. She saw the open French doors where the sheer curtain blew lightly in the breeze. The intruder stood, her feet apart, hand on the hilt of her sword and looked about. Her gaze travelled back slowly to Justina, who had by now had backed up to the bed and clung to one of the four posters for support. The blond woman sneered in disgust at the cringing woman. She spied the blue box on the duchess. She strode across the room contemptuously pushing Justina out of the way. The woman squealed as she fell back across the bed. She lay there as tears ran down her face fighting the urge to cry, especially in front of this thieving woman. The woman stopped at the duchess lifting off the top of the box. She looked at it appraisingly and casually threw it to the side, the lid, more crystal than stone or wood shattered on the mosaic covered stone floor. The thief took the small crown triumphantly from the silk lined box.

Justina screamed, "That is mine you filthy thieving whore!"

With that she scrambled onto the bed and took three lunging steps, diving at the woman, who turned upon her cry and stood staring in disbelief. She dropped the crown and it clinked on the hard wooden dresser top as Justina leapt from the bed. The intruder frantically tried to draw her short sword, but Justina was on her knocking the blade from her hand as it cleared the scabbard. They crashed against the chest of drawers and the woman grunted as she hit hard. Well, her body made the appropriate moves, but no sound came from her gasping mouth. Both women crashed to the floor amidst the broken crystal lid.

Justina went berserk. All her fears since waking, the nightmares that haunted her last night and the shattering knowledge of who she had been and what she had done came spilling to the surface in one violent rush. The thieving woman never stood a chance. Justina sat astride her, her knees in the soft part of the woman's upper arms, and leaning forward on them made the intruder grimace in pain. However all that changed as Justina, using her fists, began to beat the woman. She hit hard and fast, screaming her anger and pain with each punishing blow. The intruder tried to protect herself but Justina's fury just smashed aside the feeble defense. When the initial anger passed and the woman lay there dazed, her torn face bloody, her nose broken and her lips split and ragged. Justina saw the fallen sword and leaning over tried and pull it to her without losing her advantage. It wasn't working; the damnable blade was just out of reach. Justina gasped in frustration as her fingers scraped along the hilt. She had to shift some of her weight. The thief in desperation shoved her right knee and succeeded in toppling Justina against the duchess. The woman staggered to her feet and hit Justina in the back of the head with her hands clenched together. Justina fell forward and the woman ran, staggering from the room. Justina still in the grips of madness grabbed the sword and ran in pursuit, screaming her vengeance.

* * *

The Gathering

Alex moved slowly along the trail heading to Justina's Sanctuary. He had been pushing Jenny hard to get back to the woman he had left a few hours ago. He paused at the edge of the forest bordering his Sanctuary. He caught movement along one of the game trails he had followed to Stackit's. He took out a small metallic white colored tube and pulled. The two pieces slid out and Alex looked through it and settled the long glass on the riders. He grunted seeing Devron and Stackit along with a woman. They were about an hour from Justina's place. The riders were in no hurry so even though something important had happened, it was obvious that there was no urgency. Alex swung back to the woman. He uttered a small gasp. He took in her clothing, the hat and the tack of the horse. He was sure the strange woman was an outsider. Since he hadn't been 'informed' about her arrival, she hadn't shown up in the usual fashion that Devron, Stackit and himself had. He centered on her face, and could see she rode easily, and chatted animatedly with Stackit. He uttered a short whistle in surprise. He hadn't seen that face in almost four hundred years. It was one of the few times he had been stupid enough to get caught in the wastelands. A group of Shadow Elves were taking him back to the camp when they literally ran into this woman. The Elves went off in pursuit with a hue and cry and Alex found himself totally forgotten. He didn't hesitate and took off in the opposite direction. Now that the woman was here he had a good idea she was somehow connected with the girl he had seen all those years ago. He slid the long glass together and replaced it in his bag.

"Jenny, it looks like we might finally be getting some answers."

Jenny twitched her ears and then went on grazing. Alex gently prodded the mare and rode out to catch up to the others.

The three riders pushed along at a steady pace. Stackit and Sandra talked as they rode, even though the hunter's eyes were never still. It was actually Stackit and not Devron that saw Alex approaching.

"Hold up, I can see Alex coming."

Devron grunted in exasperation, miffed the human had seen the rider not him. He shaded his eyes with his hand.

"Yes, the human kah-bore."

Sandra looked at Devron. "What does that mean?"

"Frog creature." The rider said disdainfully.

Sandra looked at Devron incredulous. She wasn't sure if the frog slur or the human affront was worse. She had never met a man so haughty and arrogant.

Stackit had told her earlier, 'The man can't help it. He is a High Elf. They consider everyone, even the other elf clans no better than outsiders.'

"Stackit here tells me that you were once a paladin. I have never heard that name before but what Stackit has described, is some kind of holy warrior."

"I serve the blessed Nimm Bare-ehth." He said bowing to her.

"If you are so scornful of humans, why do you do me the honorific?" she asked her tone cold.

Devron noticed the change in her voice. "All women, be they fairy kin or outsider are honored."

Sandra leaned forward, her voice cutting, "If you can't be courteous to others around you, you can shove the attitude to me up your ass."

Devron flinched, never before in his life had he ever been talked to in such a manner. To make it worse, it was a human who demeaned him.

"You are lucky that honor doesn't allow me to take satisfaction on a woman." He glared at her.

Sandra laughed; the man was actually trying to intimidate her. For the first time in years she felt in control. The 'accident', which sent her to this world, had strengthened her beyond her wildest dreams.

"Mister, any time you want to try and take me on, you're welcome to try."

Devron was about to reply when Nimm Bare-ehth's voice echoed through his mind 'There is a woman, some miles from here. To gain my forgiveness you must gain hers.' Devron paused, could it be this woman was the one Nimm Bare-ehth referred to. Then the thought that had been niggling at him since the combat with the Shadow Elves began to come through more forcefully. Maybe it wasn't any one single woman per say, but all humans, outsider. He sank back onto Sabula's saddle. Cellerun had often told him that the High Elf people were too arrogant and prideful. Was this Nimm Bare-ehth's way of changing his thinking, even his very heart? Devron had to admit, that here in this 'world' there was no High Elf kingdom. It was likely that he would never see another elf as long as he lived. If this revelation was true, he had to learn to get along with others or this world and his stay here was going to be a sad, long and lonely one.

Devron looked around as he heard the sound of a woman's light musical voice laugh gently.

The four riders covered the last few miles quickly. There had been surprisingly few words said when Alex rode up. Even though she knew it was rude Sandra couldn't help but stare. At one point Stackit dropped back to make sure they weren't being followed. Alex pulled his horse in beside Sandra.

"I am so sorry that I'm staring. A lot of things have happened since I have come here and I am still trying to adjust to them. If I cause you any embarrassment I am truly sorry," she said earnestly.

Alex waved it away. "Forget about it my dear. I just hope now that you are here this place might get better. Do you have any idea what is happening?"

Sandra thought about the letter. "I have an idea, but I want to think on it a bit longer."

Alex nodded content with her explanation and they rode the rest of the way in companionable silence, even if he did catch Sandra watching him now and then.

The woman watched Alex, the half man half frog creature would have sent her to the nearest mental institution a week ago, now he didn't even faze her. She looked as the miniature-winged horse glided in and land sedately on Sultan's hindquarters. Yes, she certainly had changed. She wondered if she was anything like the scared and terrified woman who wrote the letter, or the woman who had fled the passenger lounge in Antarctica where the marines had been brutally murdered, leaving her best friend, Laura to Eric's tender mercy. Sandra shifted uneasily in her saddle wondering how her newfound confidence would affect future events, or the more chilling thought stabbed deep, maybe she had already changed the course of things to come.

* * *

The Night

The riders pulled to a stop in front of Justina's home. They all slowly dismounted and milled about waiting for Alex. He moved stiffly and had trouble getting down from Jenny. Sandra hurried over to help while the Devron, much to everyone's surprise, swiftly moved to help as well.

"Sorry to be such a pain, while my body is mostly human the muscles are not what they used to be. So many hours riding in the saddle are hard on me."

"It's okay." Sandra said as she too moved with difficulty. "I always thought I was in pretty good condition, but even I'm sore."

Devron bore most of Alex's weight while Sandra held the mare's head to stop her from moving about.

"I can see to the horses, if you would like to go inside." Devron replied formally, his tone stiff. Alex and Sandra were astonished that he was even helping at all. At least he was making an effort to fit in.

"Devron …" The paladin looked at Sandra. "… Thank you." She replied sincerely.

He smiled politely, and bowed to the woman. The congresswoman could swear there was pain reflected in his eyes.

Alex was already moving up the shallow steps and passed quickly through the door, Sandra following close behind. They stopped and looked around. The frogman let out a cry of outrage and as quickly as possible sprinted up the stairs, holding the dangling blade away from his legs so he wouldn't fall. Sandra could see a woman sprawled on the floor, her back leaning against the wall, at the top of the stairs.

Alex paused for a few seconds and could see the bloody trail from the bedroom, the tiled floor smeared up to where Justina leaned against the wall. Her feet were cut up badly and she had lost a lot of blood.

"Keep that bloody bitch away from me!" She gasped, reaching for the short sword that lay by her side.

Sandra stopped short and stayed outside the injured woman's reach.

"It's okay." Alex said soothingly. "This woman is not the one who has been causing the problems. With any luck she will be the one to fix it."

Justina glared at Sandra for a minute more, then allowed Alex to take the wavering sword. "Okay, if you say so." She grimaced.

Alex looked at her torn and bleeding feet. They were pretty messed up.

"Sandra, in the second room along the landing you will find a small box with a leather strap, bring it to me!" Alex looked at her as he spoke. The congresswoman jumped to obey his urgent orders.

"What happened ho...?" Alex gave a cough. "What happened, Justina?"

The injured woman kept a wary eye on Sandra and then looked at the frog creature examining her feet.

"I had just woken up to some kind of noise downstairs and a woman looking a lot like the one you called Sandra, broke into my room and tried to rob me. I stopped her. Unfortunately when I ran from the room chasing her, I stepped in the broken crystal on the floor." She looked at Alex, where he tenderly cradled her leg in his lap and carefully plucked out the shards that were still embedded in her feet. "How did you know about the healing kit?"

Alex toyed with the idea of telling her who he was, but he didn't want the memory of what they had together ruined by how he looked, he only too well remembered her fainting the first time he had come here. If he could keep from slipping up, he would tell her when he had changed his body back.

"I knew you when you were younger, and your husband from when I served in the Guard."

Both looked up as Sandra's cowboy boots clumped hurriedly down the polished mahogany hallway.

"Thanks." He said swiftly taking the proffered bag.

"This is going to be a great day." Justina said in resignation as she saw the elf come through the door.

Sandra and Alex both missed the remark. "Have you seen Stackit yet?" she asked the paladin.

"No, he has not returned."

66

The hunter was four miles away, bellied up to a small hill with a few shrubs screening him from the Shadow Elves below. He had only meant to check a mile or so, but he had come across a set of footprints of a small man, or woman. His curiosity aroused he decided to investigate. It was almost three miles later he found what he sought. There would have been thirty or so of the Shadow Elves in a small clearing. They must have been the ones who had attacked the paladin and the armored rider earlier on.

"So they hadn't given up after all." He mused softly.

They had a woman tied up and had been dragging her along. Now as the sun set they stopped for the night. Soon they had a fire going and Stackit had no doubt as to the fate of the captive. He worked his way closer and could see the blond hair fall over her face as the barbarians began to work on her. From the looks of the leather get up, she was the one who had attacked them last night. He grimaced, thinking about what was coming later; the bitch deserved everything she was going to get, he backed off silently. He had actually reached the horse when he stopped. He turned savagely to look back at the small hill. He couldn't leave her to the tender mercy of the savages, even if she sorely deserved it.

"Well Stackit old boy, you had better know what you are doing."

* * *

Sandra walked outside and glanced at the sky. She wondered about how it got dark, the sun, the stars, and a few other things, since reading the letter. She walked along the gravel path and kept looking down the trail for their missing friend. Sandra stuck her hands in her back pockets and turned to head back to the house. She stopped short seeing Alex materialize out of the gloom.

"Couldn't sleep either?" she asked.

"I was just going to turn in. I wanted to make sure you were staying here. Whatever happened to Stackit will have to wait for morning. We have no idea where he is, or what has happened."

"I know. I just feel so helpless." She kicked a small stone off the walk and heard it thunk against an unseen tree. "How is Justina?"

"She is asleep. The salve from her kit will pretty much see her right in a day or two."

"You still love her, don't you?"

Alex gaped at her and started to deny it, then he caved in. "How did you know."

"I can see it as plain as the nose on your face, well maybe not at the moment." She joked. "Why don't you tell her?"

Alex's shoulders slumped. "I was thinking that myself. You are a most astute young woman. I was King Michael Ashworth. I died trying to protect my wife from Devron when he attacked my kingdom."

"The man we rode in with?" Sandra asked incredulously.

"Alex nodded tiredly. "He was a man who hunted evil and his whole life was dedicated to exterminating it. He found a weapon that had an imprisoned demon in it. The man lost his soul and everything human. I have thought long and hard on things the last thousand years and I actually feel sorry for him." His eyes hardened. "But saying that, if he hurt Justina in any way, I will kill him where he stands." Alex straightened his shoulders. "It is late and I think its time for you to turn in."

"You go ahead; I want to do a bit more thinking." She looked up at the sudden movement Alex made. "I promise you, I will be a good girl and wait for morning."

Alex nodded appreciatively. "Then I bid you a good night."

The sound of the conversation carried to the woman sitting on the balcony. She had decided the room was too stuffy and she needed some fresh air before retiring. Alex had done a good job with the healing kit and it was only a minor annoyance to walk. Justina was sitting on the balcony enjoying the cool night air when the two started talking below. She thought about making some kind of noise so they would know she was up here, but the more they talked the more she was reluctant to interfere. Poor Alex, or Michael. She had a feeling for a few days he knew more of her than he let on. Did he actually think that the frog face would put her off? The woman shrugged, she might have to start with, after all she did faint, twice the first time they had met. But now after getting to know the man inside, she was reasonably sure that she wouldn't react negatively to him. Then saying that, she wondered if she would let him kiss her or touch her any way in a sexual nature. The sad truth was that in all

68

honestly, she would probably not be that receptive. And then there was Devron; she thought she knew him when he came through the door this afternoon. It looked as if she had some thinking to do as far as he was concerned as well.

Sandra was just climbing the stairs, and paused on the wide terraced landing to look once more for Stackit when she heard the squeak of a board above her. She cautiously walked out and peered upward. She could see a figure shuffle back to the open door where the curtains blew softly out over the railing. The figure was momentarily highlighted against the room light and then the door closed and a few seconds later the light went out.

'So, you were outside. I wondered when I heard something earlier.'

Now at least Sandra hoped that Justina had something to think on, and things might at least have a happy ending there. She smiled romantically; she was a sucker for the happy ever after ending.

* * *

Stackit had found a convenient pile of dirt and with a little help from his water skin soon had all the mud he wanted. He worked his way quietly to the back of the camp. The savages had been abusing the girl for hours, he had seen her scream in tortured agony, but even then she never uttered a word. Now it was late, after the witching hour and the Elves had settled down for the night. They had left two guards and even as he watched, one of them staggered over to her and urinated all over the woman. She squirmed in agony as the ammonia in the liquid made her raw wounds unbearable. The man died silently as the arrow caught him in the throat. He collapsed and lay still. The woman looked wide-eyed around. Stackit crept silently forward, angling toward the other guard. The second elf came toward her and picked up a burning stick from the fire. He staggered, sucking on his wineskin. As he passed, Stackit and his knife were as silent as they were deadly. The woman looked fearfully at the hunter and she started to squirm, fighting her bonds. It was an easy matter for him to apply a simple hold around her neck making her pass out. He quickly cut her restraints and then bending, slung her over his shoulder, swiftly made his way back to the horse.

* * *

Sandra, bleary eyed, made her way down the stairs. She looked at Alex and followed silently. He had simply said she was wanted downstairs. She had quickly pulled on her sheepskin coat that came to her upper thighs. The tiled floor was cold on her bare feet. She tagged along behind Alex as he went into the dining room, and stopped in stunned surprise. Stackit stood there giving her a little wave and smiled, when she came inside rubbing her eyes. One of the fractured personalities was sitting in the room, tied hand and foot. From the looks of her dress she was one of the ones she hadn't seen before.

"I found this piece of work after she had been captured by the Shadow Elves. I thought she was the one who attacked us last night."

Sandra looked at the badly beaten woman; she was dressed in black leather breeches and a sleeveless vest.

"Justina was attacked, and robbed earlier this afternoon. From the looks of her, she fits the description."

"What are we going to do with her? I'm sorry about bringing her here, but I couldn't leave her to the savages. Do we really have to do what the armored girl said and dispose of her?" Stackit asked quietly.

The two men looked at Sandra, and for the first time she was faced with the hardest decision of her life. She had to determine if someone was to live or die.

"All the personalities have to be gotten rid of. But I simply can't kill her in cold blood," Sandra's voice was strained with the anguish she felt.

"Can she be wished away, like the other girl?" Alex asked hopefully.

He recognized the reason for Sandra's distress, and was trying to find a way to make things easier for her. Stackit looked at Sandra and nodded hopefully.

"We can try, there is nothing to lose," She said unconvinced.

Sandra, aware she had preciously little on under her coat, carefully knelt in front of the injured girl. She was hard pressed to do nothing about easing the girl's pain. Greed looked at her and whimpered silently, using her legs, she tried to scoot away from

70

Sandra. The wounded girl looked at Sandra with a range of emotions from defiance, fear to despair. Even if she was only a copy, the girl didn't want to die.

"Shhhh, I am not going to hurt you. I might even be able to help with the pain. You have to trust me," Sandra cooed soothingly.

The woman still tried to escape, and Stackit simply propped his foot up on her shoulders stopping her. Sandra reached out, and grasped her hand tightly; the other woman jerked her hand away as if she had been burnt. Sandra held tightly as the woman fought to get away. The Congresswoman furrowed her brow, and concentrated. Greed whimpered even more, and she began to thrash around violently. Alex jumped forward and pinned her legs; Stackit had to hold down her shoulders. Sandra leant forward struggling hard to hold onto Greed's hand. With the two men holding her down, the personality splinter had nowhere to go. Sandra concentrated harder, and suddenly, Greed stiffened, panic and fear flashed across her face. Sweat broke out on Sandra's forehead. Suddenly the copy stopped moving, sinking to the floor, her face losing all the tension. For a second the splintered personality looked up at the congresswoman, and unsteadily groped for her hand. Sandra caught it and gave a reassuring squeeze, and then Greed sank back with a sigh. She shimmered for a few seconds, and then collapsed in on herself. Tears welled in Sandra's eyes as the woman began to dissolve, and then there was only dust drifting about the room. Sandra stood, swaying with emotion and then she turned and started up the stairs.

She paused, still staring straight ahead. "I need to think," she said quietly.

*   *   *

Sandra woke the next morning and lay all snuggly warm, thinking. Her mind wandered from this harsh world, to the future of her own, and then to Richard. She knew very little about the laws of physics and nothing at all about time and relativity. She lay there thinking that if she resigned, and married Richard, then maybe the planet might survive. But then she knew with an ache in her heart, no matter what she did, the future couldn't be changed. She had seen enough movies like the Terminator to know that 'fate' had a way of fixing anything she might do. Sandra turned over and tightly closed her eyes. She didn't know what to do anymore. She was tired of the responsibility. Having to make Greed go away was the hardest thing she ever had to do. Tears flooded her eyes; she was going to have to do it at least three more times.

She sat up in bed. "Damn, get hold of yourself. Cut the waterworks and the pity party," She told herself savagely.

She swung her feet out of bed, and sat there, her head hanging. Sandra heard a knock at the door, and was almost on the verge of saying 'come in' when she looked up, surprised seeing a mirror that wasn't there last night, and seeing her reflection. All she was wearing was her panties. She normally wore a fashionable nightie. Last night all she cared about was getting in bed. Now, she could see her clothes scattered across the floor.

"Who's there?" she said sighing. It was about to start again.

"Justina, I wanted to know if you wanted a nice hot bath."

Sandra pulled the sheet across her body, and shuffled to the door. She opened it and peered around, and, then let her in. Sandra sighed, rolling her eyes; a hot bath would be absolute heaven.

"I know the last few days, when I have been sorely troubled, soaking in the tub is a welcome relief."

Justina was elegantly dressed, a beautiful stylish gown, of blue velvet. The off the shoulder design showed her graceful, lovely figure. Her hair was down and she looked regal standing there.

Sandra sighed gratefully. "A bath would be heaven, and then maybe I can get some clean clothes."

Justina said shyly, "There is one matter I would like to talk to you about when you are ready."

Sandra shuffled down the hall in her sheepskin coat; let herself in the door Justina had told her of. She stared and started to giggle inanely, Sandra fought to get her mind under control. The poor house must have had a field day trying to get all the twentieth century plumbing working. The big porcelain tub sat on four little clawed feet, and the elegantly curved classical fixtures graced the tub. Sandra simply threw her coat on a bench, and slid into the water.

"Yikes, that's hot," she yelped.

Sandra sank down, and a prolonged sigh of relief slowly escaped her lips. She closed her eyes and settled deeper into the high backed bathtub, now all she needed was a bottle of wine. She peered about with one partly opened eye, and spotted a stand with a wineglass, and the bottle sitting beside the tub. Somehow without knowing why, she knew the refreshments would be there. Sandra gave a little shrug, well why not.

The Congresswoman walked down the corridor to Justina's room. She had returned to her room, one bottle later to find the bed made, and her clothing sitting folded on the bedspread. Everything was clean and fresh, her jeans, shirts, her bra and two pair of silk underwear. Now feeling immensely better, and slight tipsy she stopped at the door, and knocked gently. Justina opened the door carefully and seeing Sandra reached out to pull her inside. She pointed to the folded clothing on the bed, an exact duplicate of what Sandra wore.

"When Alex told me that we might have to ride somewhere, I wanted some clothing like yours. They seemed more practical than what we wear. What's this?" she held up the lace bra, confused as to its function.

The two women descended the stairs a short time later. Both were wearing the denim Levis. Sandra wore the long sleeved button shirt, while Justina had the short sleeved light chambray shirt. She had elected to wear the soft knee high boots instead of the cowboy boots Sandra customarily wore. Justina wiggled about uncomfortably, and pulled at the elastic strap at her side.

"You get used to it, trust me," Sandra said impishly.

"I can see how it would be a good idea, but it isn't very comfortable." She rubbed her hand up and down the seat of her pants. "I love the underwear though."

They walked across the tiled entryway, and found the others in the dining room. They looked up, staring as the two girls walked in.

"I asked The House for something practical to wear like Sandra had. This is what I got," She replied demurely.

Alex stood and smiled dreamily. "You look beautiful."

Justina blushed deeply and smiled coquettishly. "Are we going somewhere? Alex said to dress for riding."

"That will be my fault." Sandra handed the other woman the letter, and sat in a chair seeing an empty spot where bacon and eggs and a small steak waited.

Justina quickly read the letter, looking at Sandra critically when she came to certain parts.

"Okay. It would be my guess that we are going to help this SR, and you want me to try and cure whatever is making her sick."

Sandra looked up astonished. This was no empty headed woman. She grasped the situation very quickly.

"Alex said you were something of a healer before you were married to the King, and you continued on for some years," Sandra said as she paused cutting her steak.

Justina stood quietly, watching Alex; her green eyes making him squirm. She turned slightly to Sandra, side on to Alex, pulling her dark brown hair into a ponytail, deliberately exaggerating the movements of her arms, making sure her shirt was pulled tight. Justina felt her heart flutter as she glanced at Alex. What was the matter with her, she was no bloody schoolgirl. She still felt the fire in her stomach, and grimaced as it moved to her loins. She hesitated, suddenly wishing she were somewhere else. She moved to the table, and Alex hastily scooted over to her, pulling her chair out for her.

"Thank you, good sir," she purred flirtatiously, her eyes demurely downcast.

She paused as she sat before her breakfast, and glanced curiously at the man who returned to his seat. She was acting like a mare in heat around him. After over hearing the conversation of last night, she could accept that Alex was her Michael. That would explain why she felt safe around him, and why she was having these crazy feeling. Her mind would have been taken back to a time where the memories were happy, and once again she was able to relax near him. Justina wanted to encourage, even indulge the wanton feelings that had been subtly building, allowing her to fantasize about the frog/man. Suddenly it dawned on her; she didn't care in the least if he looked as he did. She wasn't sure about the kissing part, but as she watched him last night, some of the ideas she toyed with could

74

only be described as scandalous. But she didn't care anymore; it had been a long, long, long time since she had been with anyone and kissing was the last thing she was after. She knew her husband had been dead a thousand years, Justina 'knew' Alex was her husband, she felt the same wild abandonment around him. She had caught herself last night watching his tight little bum as he walked around. Michael always had the cutest little tush. If she hadn't overheard Alex confirming for Sandra who he was, Justina's own instinctive reactions would have made her realize who he was, eventually. She felt herself blush again, and pulled her thoughts back on the matter at hand.

"We still need to find the other personalities. Anyone got any bright ideas?"

Stackit squirmed in his seat. "I can think of one."

* * *

The Trap

The sun was slowly setting, and Stackit sat on the front porch, feet up on the railing, smoking his pipe. He wasn't sure about this. The one person he wanted to be waiting for was hiding in the forest. Stackit found he thought a lot about Sandra. He didn't know if it was because he was reasonably certain about how she looked without her clothes; the other woman literally had nothing to hide. He suspected it was more than that. He actually found himself jockeying to ride beside her. He liked the way she moved, the different way she smelled. Everything about the woman was like an elixir. It was a real wonder that he wasn't looking forward to the other girl arriving. After all, they were the same one, right? As soon as the thoughts seeped into his mind, he savagely discarded them. Sandra was nothing like the girl who lusted after him. Stackit knew if he hadn't been here the first night she had showed up, any man would have done. With a sigh Stackit stood, wishing it had been someone else.

* * *

Sandra and Devron hid in the shadow of the forest. The elf was actually making an effort to be civilized. No longer did he sigh whenever he was near her. He was making a genuine attempt to be accepted by the others as well, especially Alex. Sandra was a little surprised that he made no effort to be near Justina. The Congresswoman had overheard the snippets of a conversation one night about how his goddess, wanted him to get some woman's forgiveness. It must be because of Alex. There had been definite tension between the two, but that even seemed to be easing. She leaned back on the small bank, and glanced through the binoculars focused on the cabin.

* * *

Alex and Justina were likewise hidden, watching Stackit's cabin. Originally she was to go with Sandra, but she quickly volunteered to go with Alex. Now, lying beside him in the dark her body burned with a fierce fire. She could feel his body heat as he lay beside her, both watching the cabin. Justina wanted him to just rip her new clothes from her body, and take her here and now. She didn't want soft comfort; she wanted it in the dirt and rough. But what would Alex think if she even remotely suggested anything of the sort. She could feel his breath on her cheek as he turned to whisper to her. She stifled a whimper and lay, defeated, face down on her crossed arms. She didn't know if she could make such a drastic move. But then she reasoned; he was her husband.

Alex, too, was finding the close proximity hard to handle. She wasn't the only one having wild ideas. Alex dreamed of the same type of thing, however in his fantasy he was considerate, catering to her every whim. He actually heard her whimper, and was suddenly concerned. He turned to ask if she was all right. He hovered there momentarily, watching her beautiful face, the way her eyes glistened in the moonlight, how the moisture on her lips lingered when she licked them. He felt the burning in his body; he felt himself respond and embarrassed, he quickly turned on his stomach.

Justina sighed with relief when Alex turned to talk to her, and she felt the fire burning in his body, his hardness sticking in her side. She closed her eyes silently thankful.

Suddenly Alex said, "There is movement at the cabin. We can move forward now."

"Nooo, we can't!" she wailed.

Alex looked at her in real concern. "Is something wrong?"

"You know damn well there is. I could feel the way your body was hard and ready. You wanted me as badly as I want you!" she said angrily.

"You want me, Justina? I look horrible." His head sagged, "No woman would want me," he said hopelessly.

Justina turned to sit on her knees, slowly unbuttoning her shirt. Alex looked at her astonished.

"Don't worry about being gentle. Even though I haven't had a man in years, I don't want you to stop, even if I cry out."

She knew there wasn't a lot of time for them, but she didn't want to be made love to, she wanted sex, pure and simple. Alex disrobed, still feeling self-conscious as Justina slid out of her jeans.

They were soon naked under the pale moon and she lay back on the grass and pulled Alex on top of her. She groaned, as she felt his hardness between her legs. She spread them further; leveling her hips slightly as Alex entered her, sliding deeper. She clenched her eyes tightly shut, and shaking her head from side to side, stifled a painful scream as Alex pushed past her natural resistance, the pain disappeared as she was filled with the most incredible feelings.

She groaned her breasts hot against his chest panting. "Do it … hard."

Alex's hips moved rhythmically, thrusting deep into her body. His hands found her firm breasts, and his fingers squeezed her engorged nipples. She bit her lips to prevent herself from screaming in ecstasy, as her hips ground into him, riding the wave of frantic feelings that surged through her, biting on to her hand to stifle any more cries. Alex could feel himself nearing the peak, his movements became more uncontrolled; he moved frenziedly inside her, and she couldn't help but join him. He felt so good, she wanted it to go on, but Justina could feel him building for release. She threw her head back screaming silently as she orgasmed. Alex stiffened, trying not to moan out loud as he felt replete, laying quietly, cradled by her supple body. Justina was grateful he didn't try and kiss her the first time. She sighed in contentment, and cuddled him to her naked breasts, her long shapely legs twined round him. Justina smiled happily as she could fell him still moving. She stroked his back, dragging her nails lightly across his skin.

"Next time we can take it slower. I needed things this way this time," she whispered softly in his ear. "I think we should be going, the last thing we want is for anyone to come looking for us."

"Are you okay about this? I'm… I'm not the best looking man there is," he asked worriedly.

"Shhh, it's okay. At the moment it's a physical want I needed filled, but I can assure you, I do have feelings for you. I'm not sure how strong they are. But time will tell."

Alex slowly dressed, he was ecstatic, she cared for him; he had never hoped that she would in his present condition. She struggled with the unfamiliar zip her jeans had. Taking advantage of her distraction Alex moved behind her and reached around and gently ran his fingers over her stomach. She leaned into his body, getting a cuddle. Suddenly they heard the call of Devron. He longed to kiss her, but didn't want to risk ruining the moment. But as the questing voice drew closer, he pulled himself together.

"Be right there!" he called back.

Alex bent to recover the rest of his clothing. In the end Justina had to get Alex to hook the unfamiliar bra together for her.

Alex muttered appreciatively as he helped her with the little hooks, "I like this holder thing, and the silk underwear is terrific the way your skin under it feels." He coughed lightly and said awkwardly, "If this doesn't happen again, I will understand."

"M…Alex, don't worry. I am happy about what happened, and if what I think Sandra is worried about, happens. Then there will be no problems, and I will be glad of our time together." Suddenly she had a strange thought, "I don't want you to think badly of me, I wouldn't jump into 'bed' with just anyone." She had better shut up before she said too much.

She pondered the slip of the tongue; she had almost called him Michael, but if he wanted to wait for his appearance to be fixed, she wasn't going to object. It felt so good just to have him back, even it he was a little funny looking. She leaned over and kissed him on the cheek. It wasn't the most pleasant thing, but it wasn't as bad as she feared. Given time she might actually get used to it.

* * *

Stackit closed the door gently behind him. Part of him hoped the woman wouldn't show up. He stood there wondering if he should take his boots off, and try and relax when he heard the slight squeak of the loose board on the porch. He rubbed his temples; at least she didn't make him wait long. He stood and faced her as she carefully slipped through the door. She stood provocatively before him, just as she did each time. He felt as though he had been kicked in the stomach, she looked so much like Sandra. He actually contemplated taking her to bed one last time. He was reasonably sure that would be the closest he would get to the real woman. She slowly and seductively undid the tie on her leather halter, and then she moved letting it fall away. Stackit found he actually was stepping away from her, and reaching out at the same time. Suddenly he heard the pounding of booted feet on the steps, and the wooden door flung open. The woman frantically looked around, and leapt for the window in startled flight. Stackit simply stuck out his foot, and she fell heavily to the floor. Sandra and Devron rushed in grappling with her. The captive woman looked at the hunter, imploring him to help. He shook his head angrily, and bolted outside. Devron looked at Sandra, his eyebrows raised. Sandra just shrugged, but inside she was reasonably sure why he disappeared. She thought it likely that he was sweet on her, and these copies were just confusing the issue.

Sandra joined him on the porch a few minutes later.

"Is it over?" he asked, his voice a hoarse whisper.

Sandra nodded sadly. She looked up startled seeing a tear trickle down his cheek. She patted his folded arm, feeling his muscles tense at her touch. Sandra froze confused, and withdrew her hand; it was as if she had touched a hot stove.

He turned to her, kneading his eyes. "Sorry, I know it's not your fault."

Sandra replaced the hand on his arm. "Do you want to talk about it?"

He shook his head miserably. "We both know what is happening; there is no use denying it. We both feel something for the other; but we can't do anything about it, because we know one of us has ties elsewhere."

Sandra nodded, tiredly leaning her forehead on his arm. "You're right. You are so much like Richard that at times I can barely convince my wants and desires … otherwise."

"Each time one of the copies 'dies'; it's like seeing you dead. This Richard, does he know what a lucky man he is?" Stackit whispered forlornly.

Sandra smiled sweetly. "That's a nice thing to say, but the sad truth is, I'm not sure. He has his life and I mine. We live and work in separate cities, in different parts of the country. We have a comfortable arrangement. We joke that we're too old, and set in our ways to change."

Stackit turned on her almost bitterly. "Then bloody well do something about it. I can't lose you too many more times." His face sobered, and whitened as he staggered, "What if I'm a copy of the Creator's imagination as well?"

Sandra looked at Richard, err Stackit, and her heart felt for him. She craved to hide in his arms, and let him make everything all right, her body ached for his touch and she toyed with the idea of actually having one time with him, but that wouldn't be fair to either of them. She was actually reaching for him, when she stopped.

Suddenly she pulled back. "What did you say?"

"What if I'm a bloody copy of the Creator's imagination as well?"

Sandra sobered as if a cold bucket of water had been poured over her. She was confused now, if the Original Sandra subconsciously copied her own personality for some reason, maybe her fevered delirium did the same with Richard, she did after all name the mountains she lived near, The Danby Mountains.

The two were saved any further awkwardness as she spotted Alex and Justina walking across the small clearing. They stopped before the two.

"You get her?" Alex asked.

Sandra nodded. "It's late, I think it would be best to stay here the night, and leave in the morning. Do you guys mind getting the horses?"

"Not a problem," Stackit said, and he followed the frog man back to the trees.

Sandra reached up, and deftly plucked a leaf from Justina's hair. She blushed deep red.

"You okay?" Sandra asked genuinely concerned.

Justina beamed. "Yes, I think I sorted out a few things this evening."

Sandra smiled thinly; she was glad things turned out all right for someone tonight.

* * *

Stackit bustled about the small kitchen; he made pancakes for the group, and they wolfed them down, famished. None of them had eaten last night, too keyed up worrying about capturing Lust. Now breakfast was over, Stackit was tidying up the morning's mess while the two men saddled the horses. Justina was packing the food they might need over the next couple of days.

Sandra approached Stackit. "You alright?"

The man nodded, watching Justina leave the cabin with the food bags. "I feel better; I think I needed to get what I said off my chest."

Sandra paused uncertain. "Stackit, if things weren't so grave the next few years for my planet, and I didn't have some kind of future with Richard, I would be quite willing to stay here with you," she said softly, her voice husky with emotion.

Stackit impulsively grabbed her shoulders, and pulled her to him. His kiss was long and tender. She felt herself falling into his embrace. She reached for his neck, and returned the kiss with all the confused pent up emotion she had. Sandra moaned as his questing hand explored her body, fumbling with the button on her shirt, she whimpered, her breathing came in ragged gasps. He fumbled for her belt as she felt thing happening, and Sandra frantically looked over his shoulder hoping someone would come in, yet fervently praying no one would. She found herself moving back toward the bed, gently propelled by Stackit. They stopped as the footstep on the wooden porch broke the spell. She hastily stepped back, and Stackit quickly picked up his pack, hiding the obvious problem he had, and darted out past Justina. The woman stopped, and looked confused as Stackit darted past. She quickly turned to Sandra who leaned against the bed, her face flushed, and her breathing rapid. Sandra quickly fixed the top two buttons of her shirt, retightening her belt. Justina couldn't help but see the engorged nipples prominently displayed through Sandra's clothing.

"My poor girl," Justina said sympathetically, reaching out with her arms open wide. She pulled Sandra close.

Sandra buried her face in the other woman's shoulder.

"It will be okay. I know exactly how you feel." She gently patted Sandra's back.

"Alex?" Sandra asked her voice husky.

Justina nodded.

Sandra went on, "I get so confused when I'm around him. I know he's not Richard, but sometimes I want him in the worst way."

"Do you have a commitment to Richard?" she asked softly. "Do you still take different lovers?"

"I don't know about Richard, I have once. I was out with friends, and I got very drunk, I woke up with another man. I never felt so guilty in my life," Sandra confessed.

"Well, that's your answer then." Justina smiled knowingly.

Sandra laughed sardonically. "What … get drunk?"

"If it will ease your conscience, but I think you know what I mean."

* * *

The horsemen moved over the game trail pushing into unfamiliar terrain. Alex was in the lead with Stackit riding rear guard. They had been in the saddle now for hours, and each person was silent, lost in their own thoughts. The diminutive pegasus swooped overhead, Sultan would whinny to him from time to time. Sandra decided to call him Rocky, after the flying squirrel from the Bullwinkle TV show that was still being rerun on the late night cable channel. Sandra was very aware that Stackit was avoiding her. So she dropped back till she was riding with him. His face lit up momentarily as she pulled next to him, but then quickly resumed the melancholy look. She rode for a while beside him, just enjoying his company. She had been thinking long, and hard on what Justina had said, finally she came to a conclusion.

"Stackit, you have made this very difficult." He started to defend himself, but stopped when she held up her hand. "I want you the worst way at times, and your appearance is one of the things that puts me off. I'm just as confused over you, as you are about me. But I will not fight things anymore. If something happens like this morning, then I will happily let it." Sandra finished off softly, her voice husky with her emotion.

Stackit just stared. "I thought you might hate me for being so bold and taking advantage of you. I know this is confusing, and if I'm completely honest with you, I kind of hoped that this morning, that you would be so worked up, you wouldn't care about things. That wasn't fair, and I'm sorry."

She reached out and gently laid her hand on his, resting on the saddle pommel. "Let's just take things slowly. The situation may not come up again, or we may all be dead in the next day or so. In the meantime I value you too much too have you mad at me."

"Come on people, keep up!" Alex roared, seeing the couple lagging behind. After last night with Justina he had a vague idea what was bothering the young couple. Sandra and Stackit, gently spurred the horses, and quickly caught up.

The small cavalcade wound its way along the game trail, climbing steadily higher into the pass. They rounded the corner and the little flying horse was sitting in the middle of the path. Alex moved out around him, and then pulled up short as the pegasus shifted sideways blocking the way.

"Sandra, this creature is blocking the way," Alex called back.

She dismounted; shucking the rifle, working her way past the other mounts. Stackit followed, and handed the reins to Justina. The woman stopped seeing Rocky; the little flying horse winging off, and darted down the trail dodging the trees. They moved slowly for a minute, and then came out on the tree line looking into the valley beyond the pass. Sandra slid behind a convenient rock, leaned the rifle against the stone, and unwound the binocular straps. She surveyed the landscape below.

After a minute of quartering the woods Sandra said tightly, "Shadow Elves." She swept further on. "I see a dead horse, there looks to be arrows in the side."

"You can see all that from here?" Stackit gasped impressed.

She smiled and carried on looking. She swept back quickly having passed over something. "I see a woman in a white dress. She is wading along the riverbank. She looks to be hiding among the foliage."

"Let me guess, she looks a lot like you and the other copies?" Stackit asked.

84

"She isn't one I have seen before, maybe she is Hope, or the other copy we're looking for," Sandra murmured.

"Either way, we're going to need to help her. If she is one of the copies you can do your thing, if it is Hope she might be able to take us to this woman you're looking for," Stackit whispered tightly.

"Okay, can you work your way down? I'll tell the others and cover you from up here."

Stackit nodded grimly.

Sandra reached out. "Don't get caught," she said her voice full of concern.

He leaned over and kissed her lightly, then disappeared over the side.

* * *

The water was cold against the woman's bare legs, and she had trouble forcing them to move. Her sandals slipped on the slimy stones, and with a gasp she sank up to her chest in the freezing stream, rushing past her. As the water surged past her stomach, her breathing came in short sharp pants. She could feel the split second of warmth as her bladder voided in the sudden icy immersion. Hope stopped, her teeth chattering, she rubbed her bright red legs, looking intently into the foliage, fearing the sudden noise might alert her pursuers. Hope slogged through the waist deep water, the sound of the savages close behind her, looking fearfully over her shoulder. There was a snap of a twig, and lunging to the bank, the woman sank under the overhanging branches, the wave of water from her lunge smacked against her face. Hope hugged the bank, mud coating her, and the white dress; she gagged on the dirty water, and retched. Pushing the wet grimy hair out of her face, her eyes wide in fear, she sank back into the water neck high, picked up a stick, and bit down trying to keep her chattering teeth apart. The tree branch above her pushed down sharply, and she heard the cry of surprise higher up. One of the warriors slipped on the bank, his leg sliding into the water. Hope looked terrified as the warrior began jabbering in some strange language. The branch snapped further, and with a yelp the man sank to his waist. The savage stared in stunned surprise as he stood face to face with the woman. Hope stifled a scream. The barbarian lunged for her, and in defense; Hope dodged backwards, the branch she was clinging to whipped forward catching the man just under the chin. He gurgled and sank to his knees. The man choked out a strangled cry, his hands frantically at his throat, his wide staring eyes fearful. His breathing became more panicked, and in desperation, Hope dived forward, her weight forcing him down. Slipping in the muck, she fell forward. Hope's head smacked into the barbarian with a massive wallop; the man's eyes turned up, and he slipped beneath the water. Clinging frantically to the overhanging branch as the world swam before her eyes, her blurry vision focused on the bubbles that even now dotted the surface. With a last forlorn lunge, Hope grabbed the branch, and weakly hauled her freezing body into the tree. Feebly climbing higher, her stunned mind tried to make sense of the cacophony of noise that assaulted her. She managed to advance a few more feet when she sank against the main trunk, exhausted and slipping into hyperthermia, she quietly passed out wedged in the nook of the tree.

* * *

Stackit paused, hiding in the rocks as the barbarian stormed past him. He looked up, to the rock face across the river trying to orient himself. He could make out Sandra. She was pointing further along. She must have been watching through that marvelous looking glass she had. The savages were upset, that much was certain. They combed the area, and returned going over the ground they already had been across. Whoever they had been following, they had lost and the men were not happy. Even now he could hear the angry shouts of the search parties.

He moved carefully, not bothering to wait. If they couldn't find the woman in the white dress, they were certainly not going to find him. Stackit moved into the shadows, becoming one with them. He had to find the woman fast. He knew that at this altitude, fast moving water was nothing short of freezing. The woman was in acute danger of dying of exposure. The hunter soon found signs where someone had gone to the water's edge and didn't return. It didn't take him long to find the broken branch sagging into the river. He edged closer and could see the brown leather jerkin of one of the savages. Unsure if he fell or what, Stackit slid up against the tree trunk, and squatted down, trying to piece together what had

86

happened. The wind lightly played the trees like a finely tuned instrument, and the hunter caught the fragrance of something familiar. He sniffed about, his nose in the air, but he was unable to pin it down. If he didn't know better he would have sworn Sandra was here. The scent that wafted hauntingly around his nose was the same ... Sandra. She had laughed one time saying it was her soap. Stackit listened intently. There wasn't a sound anywhere that was natural. The elves had left for the time being, and he reasoned the birds should have started their songs again. Something wasn't right, and he heard the tiniest creak. He raised his head slowly, and could see through the vague gloom from the overhanging willow the unnatural shape of something higher in the tree. He stifled a brief exclamation seeing a patch of white. Stackit quickly, nimble as any monkey, swarmed up the tree.

It took less than a minute to reach the woman. He sucked his breath in. She was soaked, with the water dribbling down the rough bark. Her grimy dress was molded to her body, drenched like the material was, the dress was almost see-through. Her dirty hair clung to her head and little blobs of mud marked her beautiful face. She looked ghastly, her skin was so pale, it was white, and her normal ruby lips were ashen and grey. Stackit felt as if he had been kicked in the pit of the stomach. He reached out to touch her, finding the hand cold and clammy. He shifted positions trying to get closer to her, but the awkward angle of her body made it difficult to get near. Stackit managed to get to her upper body. He touched her face, and could feel faint warmth. With a great deal of difficulty, he managed to position himself carefully, and put his ear to her breast. He held his own breath, and managed to hear a faint beat. Stackit shifted so he was straddling her, and quickly dug the rope from his backpack. He looped it around her upper body, and then wrapped the rope about a branch; awkwardly, he managed to get her body out of the crook of the tree. Stackit slowly let her slide earthward, and then propping his feet against another branch, gently lowered her to the ground. The hunter joined her a second later. He stashed the rope in the bag. Lifting her to his shoulder, her head down his back, and holding onto her grimy, slimy legs, Stackit made sure the trail was clear as he darted into the rocks.

The hunter quickly gathered the driest wood he could find, and built a number of small fires. He positioned the woman in the middle, and quickly stripped off the dress, and dug the tattered blanket from his backpack, wrapping her in it. Stackit took a few minutes to scout the area around the tree. He used every skill he knew to erase the tracks he made. He also wanted to find out how close he had to be in order to smell the smoke. He grimaced; he could smell the fire from ten feet away, fortunately the wind was blowing in the other direction. However, it couldn't be helped. If the woman was to survive she had to be warmed. The hunter returned, and reached under the blanket, and took out her arm, it was still colder than normal but at least the color was returning. He massaged her arms for a minute to help the circulation return, then moving to her feet, did the same for her legs. Stackit was very aware of how much she looked like Sandra, so he was very careful where his hands went. She moaned slightly, and he felt his heart leap. The woman was still in no shape to go anywhere.

He did another quick trip, and could find no sign of the Shadow Elves anywhere, but he knew they were crafty and canny. Their knowledge of the wilds was hard learned. Stackit took the little metal mirror out of the side pocket, and sat it on top of one of the bigger boulders propped up by a little rock. He returned to the small camp, and waited for help to arrive, and the girl to wake. As he sat there, Stackit watched the woman, she seemed to be sleeping peacefully now, and her face was a more healthy color. The hunter took the water skin and a cloth, which he wet and carefully cleaned her face and hair as best as he could. The man's touch was gentle; he had no desire to wake the woman. After he had cleaned off the mud on her legs, Stackit looked up to see her watching him carefully. He carried on as if he hadn't noticed her scrutiny, cautiously washing the other, and then tucking the blanket back around her.

Stackit knelt by her. "Thirsty?"

She looked up and nodded, smiling gratefully. He gently put his hand under her shoulder, and moved her high enough so she could drink easily, then settling back, where she drifted back off to sleep. Stackit looked at his hand where he had touched her bare skin. Her skin was so smooth, he sniffed his hand, the gentle fragrance of her skin lingered for a moment, and he couldn't help but smile.

* * *

Sandra was worried. Stackit had been gone now almost two hours. The little group in the pass was all lining the rim watching for him. There had been no movement now for almost a full hour. The elves had returned, and after an angry debate left quickly. Sandra was worried the savages had found him. But she had enough faith in the man to know the barbarians would never catch him. So he had to be hiding. Sandra extended her search, and within five minutes, found what she sought; a small bit of mirror, or metal, reflecting the sun high atop a boulder.

* * *

The horses once again were following in single file. Justine, being the smallest rider doubled with Hope after the gear was redistributed to the other mounts. Sandra couldn't help but notice Stackit was very attentive to the rescued woman. She was a bit miffed, and if she admitted it to herself, she was even a little jealous. She had made such a sweeping declaration of her heroic self-sacrifice about the man that she felt he owed her something. But, hard on the heels of that ridiculous thought, she was also genuinely glad that Stackit found Hope attractive. She grinned lopsidedly at the strange things women put themselves through over men. She was suddenly happy, even starting to whistle the song of an old movie she had liked as a little girl, 'The Wizard of Oz'. The tune of 'We're Off to See the Wizard' followed in their wake.

Hope directed them along a narrow trail that climbed higher for the best part of two hours. She informed them that this wasn't the way she normally travelled, but the Shadow Elves were getting braver, and as a result they were pushing closer to The Creator's Sanctuary. Hope had even seen Anger with the group. The riders thought on that as they rode. It seemed funny that all the other copies had been hunted, and in Greed's case had even been tortured by the barbarians.

It was late afternoon that they stopped before a sheer wall with a massive double gate built into the stones. Hope shivered in

89

the cool air; she had lost her jacket when her horse went down under her. She walked up to a smaller door set in the middle of the left half of the massive gate. Sandra looked intrigued as Hope pulled a heavy chain through a good-sized hole in the wood, and found a big weighty brass padlock. Hope took a small chain from around her neck, and using the key attached, opened the lock and the rhythmic rattle of the links dragging over wood was uncomfortably loud, echoing off the stonewall in front of them. The riders watched the surrounding area leery of attack now they were vulnerable. Dragging open the smaller door, obviously heavy to Hope's slight frame, the riders filed through, most of them bending over to clear the lintel, their knees rubbing against the frame. Hope pulled the door closed and relocked it.

They followed her as she walked a short ways, they rounded a bend, and the riders looked in dismay at the rickety suspension bridge, with the gaps between the slates dismally wide.

"We're not crossing that, are we?" Justina declared in emphatic surprise.

Hope grinned mysteriously and walked confidently over the swing bridge. It remained steady under her weight; obviously not as poorly constructed as first thought. Hope pulled the camouflaging bushes away from a small object, not clearly identifiable from this distance. She cranked swiftly, and the riders looked relieved as the cables tightened up, forcing the planks together. When Hope was finished, the bridge was sturdy enough to ride the horses across without any problem. Hope swung up, back behind Justina and pointed ahead.

"It's not far, just around that small group of trees."

* * *

90

Original Sandra

The small company waited patiently as the Creator slept peacefully. They had found her in a delirious, stressed state. The woman was thin and gaunt, her skin hot and dry as she looked at them with madness burning in her eyes.

Hope ran forward, gathered her hand to her chest with both of hers whispering excitedly, "I found them, just where you said they would be." She looked at her dearest friend, and tears welled into her blue eyes, saddened at the condition of the woman. "I'm sorry I took so long. There was trouble on the trail."

Sandra gently took her shoulders, and looked at the woman she had come all this way to meet. She was again almost a mirror image. The blond tresses were shot with grey, and the once beautiful face was tired, worn and starting to wrinkle. Her once lush hair was stringy and dirty. Sandra pulled Hope up, and moved back so Justina could get closer to her patient.

"Come on Hope, let's wait outside."

The woman grinned wanly, and nodded her understanding as Justina moved closer, putting her healing kit on the bed. As the door closed on the two women, the former queen was sitting on the bed starting her examinations.

* * *

The wait now extended to almost three hours, and Justina still had not emerged. Devron muttered something about tending to the horses, while Hope stood abruptly and left. Stackit hovered undecidedly, caught between his desire to stay with Sandra, yet wanting to see Hope.

"Stackit, if you like the girl you should go to her. As much as I would like you to stay with me, it's not fair on you or Hope. You both deserve some happiness, and if this is successful I will be returning home. Go, make some kind of future with her," Sandra said softly.

91

"Sandra..." he started, and stopped uncomfortably, then quickly nodded and stood, following the other woman.

Stackit paused outside; the beauty of the country was breathtaking. He lingered, listening to the sound of the birds, the light breeze, warm in the confines of the box canyon playing a melodic tune in the trees. He couldn't help but sigh; this was truly peaceful and quiet. He could actually like living here. The slight noise of water jerked him away from his reverie. He carried on around the building.

He could see a small stable off to the side, but he was astonished to see a big, stone-encircled body of water. The pool must be close to twenty feet long and ten wide. He gazed fascinated as he caught the blur of beige color streaking under the waves. He looked to see a white cotton dress dropped haphazardly on a wooden bench. Instinctively he understood the ramifications as the woman surfaced, her arms on the stone lip looking at him. Stackit could see she wore nothing, the rest of her upper body visible, was toned, blemish free, and incredibly desirable and as she settled on her folded arms Stackit gazed at her classically shaped face, her honey blond hair clung to her. Hope had the clearest blue eyes he had ever seen. Stackit was entranced, beguiled by the beauty, and the glow she radiated. Hope lifted herself out of the water, and Stackit couldn't help but stare at her body. As he felt himself respond to her, he quickly turned his back, suddenly embarrassed. Stackit wasn't sure why, after all he had seen Lust naked, and this girl had nothing the other copy didn't have. Stackit started as she touched him. He jumped, that wasn't true. Lust had all the wrong ideas, while Hope was peace, naivety and innocence personified.

"Is there something wrong?" Hope asked suddenly unsure. "Do you not find me attractive?"

"Oh ... yes ... I most certainly do," Stackit replied fervently, he breathed deeply to steady his racing heart. "But there are things I might need to explain to you. I think it would be better for me if you put something on."

* * *

92

Justina walked slowly down the stairs. She looked beaten, the long ride, the frantic few days since she 'awoke', and now the strain of caring for the sick woman was beginning to tell.

"She is awake, and she wants to see you," Justina replied tiredly, and then muttered, "I need something to eat."

"There is some bread on the counter, there is meat, cheese and spreads in the fridge," Sandra said absently as she started up the stairs.

Justina stared at the retreating woman, not sure what a fridge was, or what spreads were, but she wearily trudged to the kitchen, she would find out soon enough.

* * *

Sandra moved down the familiar hall, and paused at the door, to 'her' room. She shook off the eerie feeling pushing open the door that stood slightly ajar. The room was poorly lit, and from the smell of things, the woman hadn't cleaned it, bathed or changed her clothes in a while. The original Sandra lay back in her bed, propped up with a number of pillows. Already she seemed better; her skin looked more natural, not pasty and burning. The woman's eyes were clear.

"Come in, come in," she said weakly.

Sandra moved into the room and stood, unsure what to do. Original Sandra wore her Los Angeles Dodger jersey, and from where Sandra stood she could see the other woman wore nothing under her shirt. The sick woman pulled up her covers almost to her shoulders.

"Sorry about my state of undress," she muttered. "I normally don't go out without being properly presented. Except when..."

"Richard is around," Sandra finished for her.

Both women laughed a little at what had been a standing joke between her and Richard.

"I guess you have a lot of questions. What will happen to earth, how I got here, maybe a dozen others, about Richard, your career."

Sandra settled on the bed. "I do, but I don't think I want to know anything. I'm afraid that by simply having this experience has changed the way history will play out. When I came here, I was like the woman you described in your letter." She paused gathering her thoughts, "Well, I'm not that woman anymore; someone who is afraid of her own shadow. I think any more information will change things even more."

Original Sandra sat up awkwardly in bed. "Maybe things should be changed. Billions of people will die in the comet strike, and the following winter. If they can be saved, don't you think we have the right?"

Sandra looked at the other woman, staggered by what she was saying. "What about all the people that have lived since then. If history is changed, millions of people, like the races Stackit told me about, will not exist. Do I, or you for that matter, have the right to play God?"

The woman slumped back in bed. "I have already been through all that. I went over it so many times I think that's what caused the breakdown." She shook her head. "I don't think I actually want to change history … completely," she sighed tiredly. "I think I just want to redeem some mistakes I made. One or two of my decisions, by their very nature will be directly responsible for hundreds of people dying, thousands indirectly."

Sandra looked around the room. "No, I don't want to know. Look at the shit you've got me into as it is. I have to play God, deciding how a woman will die. You said that I had to be the one to get rid of the copies, what about Hope? Do I murder her as well; deprive a good man of his chance of happiness?" Sandra had risen to her feet, her face livid and angry when she finished.

Original Sandra's face dropped at Hope's name. "She is my pride and joy, my crowning achievement."

The Congresswoman stood there speechless. "What did you say?" She lunged forward causing the other woman to shrink back involuntarily. "What did you do!" she hissed tensely.

Tear spilled from the tired eyes, ran unheeded down the aging face, and pooled on the white comforter. "I had information given to me with the utmost secrecy, to be delivered to a certain scientist, in a certain underground bunker. The car taking me to the secret location was attacked. I'm not sure who or why. But I hid the documents down the back of my pants in case. An army patrol from the base found the car, I was the only survivor. When they got me to the bunker I was delirious, and unknown to me the comet had changed direction slightly, so it would hit us earlier than expected. They stabilized me and then without even cleaning me up, I was stuck in a cryo unit!" Original Sandra cried as if her heart was breaking. "I dreamed of that attack for hundreds, maybe thousands of years. I relived my driver being shot, and Major McCandel, desperately calling on the radio for help, and then he too was gunned down trying to protect us. I was vaguely conscious when the attackers dragged Virginia, my young aide from the car, and repeatedly raped her then, shot her between the eyes. Her screams and the sounds they made were terrifying. They found me, dragged me outside, and ripped open my shirt. They pawed at me, hurt me. I can still feel their mouths on my body; one licked my face. I tried to fight, scream and claw them, but I was too badly dazed by the homemade mine we had hit. One man drew his knife, and was starting to cut my belt when the army arrived. I ... have ... dreamed of ...that ... thousands ... of ... times!" she screamed every syllable.

Sandra stared at the other woman, reached forward and gently gathered her into her arms. She cooed softly until Original Sandra stopped crying.

She wearily sat back, sniffed twice, wiped her eyes on the bedding and went on, "When I woke I found I still had the reports on me. I went to see one of the scientists, and he informed me that they were the notes and research, a breakthrough in cloning technology. I learned everything I could, and later when the accident sent me here I lived for hundreds of years on my own. I found my brain could make things here, even stuff that normally wouldn't be here. I suddenly found I had electricity. I was even able to watch my old John Wayne discs and listen to U2. In the end, I decided to try recreating the technology in the reports. Everything I thought of, the house made. So you see, it was me; I made the copies coldly calculated to rid my life of the terrible loneliness. Several times I even thought of suicide, but as I found out the house doesn't care to be left alone either."

Sandra sat back thinking on what she had said. "It seems the house has a lot of your personality in it as well, and that fear of being alone was imprinted on the place. How do you know that getting rid of the copies will fix whatever is wrong in this world."

Original Sandra took a deep breath, and then sighed softly. "I don't, not for sure. It's just something I know in my head."

The woman sitting on the side of the bed abruptly stood, slowly pacing as she thought. She couldn't very well sit in judgment of her actions. Sandra knew what it meant to live in fear, and she never did like being alone for too long a length of time. Original Sandra created this mess so the Congresswoman had to trust her that she knew how to fix it.

"I'll find Anger, but I will have nothing to do with killing Hope. We will have to find another way, even if I have to take her back with me," she declared empathically.

The woman in bed pulled the blanket higher to her chin and nodded meekly.

Sandra sighed, fighting to control her voice. "We're going to figure this out. Why don't you get cleaned up, if you're able?"

* * *

Sandra descended the stairs as if in a trance. She still wasn't sure what to do. The Congresswoman gripped her fist in frustration. She wasn't even sure where the second missing girl was. She paused, seeing Justina come out of the kitchen.

"This place is amazing. That box in there is cold, and keeps perishables fresh." She held up a sandwich, "I'm not sure what peanut butter is, but I love it."

Sandra grinned and sank down on the couch, and watched as Justina came and sat beside her. They both looked up expectantly as Stackit and Hope came in, Alex just behind them.

Stackit stopped dead, seeing the ashen look on Sandra's face. "What is it? What's happened?" his face turned white, afraid to hear what they had been talking about.

Swiftly Sandra gave them a quick rundown on what the two had been talking about. Alex and Justina sat silently with their private thoughts. Stackit looked as close to anger as Sandra had seen him. Hope looked dejected and resigned.

"I'm not going to let that bloody witch upstairs play God." He looked pleadingly at Sandra. "I will not let her, or any of you hurt Hope."

The girl concerned looked sharply at the hunter, and a rather becoming blush settled over her.

"I promise you Stackit, no one is going to touch Hope." Sandra's tone brooked no argument.

"I don't want to die, but if it is what it takes to cure this world, I don't see how I have much of a choice," Hope declared weakly.

Stackit sat beside her, and gently pulled the lovely woman toward him. He held her as she trembled; she sniffled, refusing to give way to the tears that threatened. The hunter just sat there and glared at anyone who thought of harming her.

* * *

Original Sandra paused unseen at the top of the stairs, her clean clothing, and towel held close. She stifled a gasp seeing Hope, and Stackit huddled close. He sat with his arm protectively around the small of her back, and Hope cuddled close to him, her head on his shoulder. The conversation raged around the room, and in the end Original Sandra knew what must be done. She slowly descended the stairs and the talk died.

"The Shadow Elves have a camp a few miles from here. Hope can give you a map, and it will take about twenty minutes to get there." She slipped a small chain from around her neck and tossed it lightly to Sandra. "Here is the key to the gate." She looked to where a grandfather clock sat. "It is about five now, the barbarians are usually in camp. They go out again in an hour or so."

Without a word the other quickly stood and left, Sandra lingered briefly watching the other woman. She could see the gold watch on her left arm.

Original Sandra noticed her look. "It is one of the things you didn't want to know about."

The Congresswoman stood looking at the older version of herself, and nodded once. Something about her wasn't right. All the tension was gone, she looked relaxed, and in control. She had made a decision about something, and it strangely bothered the congresswoman. Again she nodded, and walked to the door. Original

Sandra waved slightly, and then moved behind her and closed the door.

Sandra had a sudden bad feeling, and she darted around the back to where the horses were kept.

"Hope, don't ask why, but I want you to wait here. I want you to keep an eye on the Creator."

Hope looked puzzled but didn't argue with the urgency in Sandra's voice. She turned, and hurried back to the house. Stackit watched her go, and then looked at Sandra warily.

"Let's get this over with, don't ask me why, but I have this feeling we have to hurry."

The other mounted up, and thundered out of the gate.

* * *

Original Sandra stood at the shuttered window watching them ride out; even as they cleared the yard she was darting out the back.

* * *

Hope came in the front door, and pausing uncertainly. She didn't know where the Creator was, or why Sandra wanted her to stay behind. She heard a creak, and swiftly moved to the back of the house finding the door open, swinging in the evening breeze. Hope looked horrified as she noticed the spare key to the gate was missing.

Hope sat on the couch, her legs drawn up beside her, and waited apprehensively. It was only the matter of minutes before the Creator rode back into the yard on her Sultan. The woman didn't even bother unsaddling the horse; she simply dismounted, and headed for the house. Original Sandra stopped seeing Hope, and with a look of pure terror across her face. She turned quickly, and wide-eyed watched the smoke rise into the evening sky.

"Why, oh why are you here?" the Creator moaned. She hurried forward and grabbed Hope roughly by the arm. "You must get away. Hurry or they will be here."

Hope looked thoroughly confused which rapidly spread to alarm when the Creator reached over the fireplace, and took down

98

her Winchester. Both women looked out of the window in alarm when they heard Sultan whinny.

"Deception," breathed Original Sandra, in dismay. "Hurry out the back door."

Hope turned as the Creator pushed her out the door. "Why? You didn't have to take the spare key. We would have found a way to fix things."

Original Sandra cupped Hope's soft face with her hand. "I love you. I made this mess, and Sandra may have been right. I should have to clean it up."

Hope was crying freely. "Did she say that?"

"No, she is still a decent woman, maybe now she will have a chance to remain one. Go my dear; tell them I am truly sorry."

They both turned quickly at the sound of the front door shuddering under a heavy boot. Original Sandra gave the girl a kiss on her forehead, and then pushed her out, and closed the door behind her. The woman then looked at the rifle, and threw it on the dining room table. She had run out of shells long ago. She didn't want Hope trying to stay. The ex-Congresswoman of Colorado picked up her towel, and carried on back up the stair whistling a happy tune.

* * *

The riders had been ten minutes out when Sandra turned in the saddle and then reined up sharply, Sultan whinnying in protest.

"Oh, for the love of God, what has she done?" Sandra breathed in resignation.

The other four pulled up as well, and turned to look where Sandra was watching. The black pillar of smoke was noticeable; anyone within ten square miles would see it.

* * *

Sandra knelt looking at the Shadow Elves that arrayed themselves between them and the Creator's Sanctuary, there was close to thirty of them, and the five companions could see Anger standing in the forefront. She looked furious, and if truth were told, the small group thought, see she looked a little desperate.

"Can you take care of these; I need to find, Original Sandra," Sandra said tightly.

Devron stood beside her; he drew himself upright, pulling his sword from the scabbard, and looked at the congresswoman. "We will not let you down." He then turned to look at the frog creature. "Michael, I would be honored to stand with you."

The man looked at the elven paladin. "I would be pleased." And then he drew his rapier.

Justina leapt forward, and wrapped her arms around his somewhat slimy shoulders. "Don't you dare go, and die on me again! I don't think I could handle it"

She picked up the bow she had dropped in her haste to get to Michael; she had never fired one of these things in anger. She had been limited to the archery range at the palace.

Stackit grinned. "Nothing to it, just pretend each of them is a little bull's eye."

Sandra nodded and hugged each person, lingering a bit longer with Stackit than she probably should. The resemblance between him and Richard was just too much. Suddenly, she resolved if she ever got home to tell him how she felt.

"I'll see you shortly," she said positively.

They looked at her steadily; each wondered who would be alive after the next ten minutes.

"Justina, you and Stackit stay here in the rocks. Keep firing on the barbarians, and when they charge we'll meet them in the narrow confines of the defile here between the two cliffs faces," Devron said.

They all nodded their affirmation, and then scattered to their positions.

Devron looked at each of them. "May Nimm Bare-ehth's blessing be upon each one of you."

*　　　*　　　*

Sandra crept closer to the Sanctuary, her trusty Winchester handy. The Original Sandra's Sanctuary looked a lot like the cabin at Black Lake. The split-level home was simple in design, and if she remembered right from the last visit, Sandra's bedroom was on the top floor, like she had in Colorado. She paused and looked back to the rock, trying to see how the group was managing as she could hear the screams of the warriors as they charged, and then the clang of steel on steel. Sandra almost faltered, and returned to help. But somewhere was the last personality they hadn't seen yet, and there was also the smoke. Sandra levered a shell into the chamber, and bent over, hurried forward. Suddenly she saw a woman burst from the house, running. She was dressed in a white knee length dress and simple sandals, her honey blond hair loose about her shoulders.

"Hope, here!" she cried, and waved for the woman to see.

The woman stopped briefly, and then spotted Sandra, sprinting for her. Sandra couldn't help but think how beautiful the woman looked in that dress, maybe she should get one when she got back.

Hope slid to a stop, and breathlessly turned, kneeling to watch the house. "She is inside."

"Deception?" Sandra asked tensely.

Hope nodded. "She must have slipped in. I heard them arguing upstairs."

Quickly the woman told Sandra about the Creator, and the extra key.

"There is nothing we can do about it now." Then what Hope just said pushed through her rapidly whirling mind. "Deception can speak?" Sandra asked sharply.

Hope nodded. "Not too well, but you can tell she has been working on it."

"Let's go," Sandra said as she rose to stand.

Suddenly the whole area gave a violent shake, and somewhere close, the two women heard a tremendous explosion and the earth gave another heart-stopping jolt.

"What in God's name is that?" Sandra asked worriedly.

She had been in an earthquake once, when the congressional fact finding mission she was on went to California. The whole northern end was devastated by one of the most destructive events in the history of the United States. San Francisco was just swallowed by the sea, as the land around it broke apart. Hope looked terrified.

"Come on, we need to help the Creator." Sandra's voice was strained.

101

Hope nodded quickly, as she too fought to control her all apparent terror.

Sandra ran for the front door, stealth no longer needed in her haste to get to the Original Sandra. Hope doggedly right behind her.

Sandra bowled the door, and tumbled through it. The frame splintered under the impact of her body. She slid unceremoniously to the floor, skidding on the polished wood. Hope stopped, looking confused as to what had happened.

"I tripped on the loose stone on the porch; my own place has it as well," she said ruefully as she clambered to her feet.

Both women heard footsteps thudding on the stairs from the upper room. Hope looked up worriedly, Sandra expecting trouble, shouldered the rifle. A woman burst from the stairwell, and looked wildly around. Sandra relaxed seeing a woman in blue jeans and a California Angels t-shirt. The thought flashed through Sandra's mind. 'I wouldn't wear that t-shirt in public.' Her team was the Los Angeles Dodgers; Richard's had been the Angels. Original Sandra wheezed, and leaned against the railing holding her neck.

"The bitch tried to cut my throat," she wheezed.

Sandra moved forward, and the other woman gently moved her hand. There was a thin line of blood across her neck, oozing nicely.

"You were lucky, any deeper and you would be dead. Is she upstairs?"

Original Sandra nodded carefully, and Sandra hastened up the short flight of steps.

Hope moved to her friend. "Are you okay?" She asked tenderly.

The woman nodded, and moved away, stepping down into the lounge. In doing so, Hope noticed her breasts jiggled with her movement. She rapidly sucked in her breath, looking at Original Sandra in surprise. The woman stared back, her eyes boring deep into Hope, suddenly she shivered. The woman in the white dress rubbed her bare shoulders, and looked at the open door. She turned and tried to close it as best as she could.

"I had better see what is happening upstairs," she said quickly.

She pushed past Original Sandra, and then leapt forward taking the stairs two at a time.

*   *   *

Sandra looked up sharply as Hope came thundering in. She stopped behind the congresswoman as she squatted on the floor, the rifle across her lap. Hope yelped unexpectedly as she stared at the dead woman. Her body was naked, but for a blue pair of panties, her long greasy blond hair sprayed over her face. They could see a torn and stained Dodgers jersey crumpled under the bed. The woman lay amidst the broken lamp that had caved the side of her head in.

"I don't understand why she is still here? The other bodies dissolved when they died. Why did she take the clothes?" Sandra mused.

"I don't think this is the copy, this is the Creator," Hope hissed through clenched teeth leaning over Sandra's shoulder.

Sandra sighed, suddenly sickened and saddened. "That would make sense," she picked up the left arm of the dead woman.

There was a thin white band on her arm where something had been strapped on. Sandra leaned over to see the discoloration more closely. She could see the tiny round area on the top of her forearm. The Original Sandra had worn a watch that Richard had given her, or would give her in a few months' time.

"That woman downstairs doesn't have a breast holder on," Hope said.

Sandra looked at her and she could see Hope was genuinely distressed.

Hope went on quickly. "The Creator would never let anyone see her without being restrained, except for..."

"Richard." Sandra finished for her. Now the t-shirt and the watch markings made sense. "The bitch!" Sandra growled.

She stood quickly, and hurried back down. Hope right behind her. Sandra reached the bottom steps and the string pulled across the hall tripped her. She fell crashing to the floor, leaving her momentarily stunned, her rifle was sent spinning off to the side. Deception was on her like a tiger savaging raw meat. A piece of rope was quickly looped around her neck, and the impostor pulled with all her strength. Sandra staggered to her knees, trying to get her fingers under the rope where it cut into her neck. She was gasping for breath, fighting all the time to stand, her eyes wide and staring. Deception put her knee in the congresswoman's back, and pulled, as her arms jerked. Sandra sagged to her knees, spots appeared before her eyes. Her head swam with a roaring sound, and then unexpectedly she dropped forward on her hands as the rope came mercifully loose.

Hope had been right behind Sandra when she fell over the trip wire. She watched them fight for a moment trying to see a way to help. She spotted the rifle off to the side, and jumped for it. Sandra was close to passing out; moments from death when Hope smacked Deception in the back of the head with the rifle butt. The woman sagged clumsily onto Sandra. Hope levered the stunned body off Sandra, and quickly loosened the constricting rope. Sandra pushed herself to her knees taking deep breaths of air. She massaged the painful burn marks on her neck. Deception launched herself screaming furiously at Hope, who went down under the onslaught. Abruptly there was a sharp crack of the rifle's retort in the confined room. Hope whimpered as Deception stiffened, the look of pained surprise etched her beautiful face. The hunting knife she had pulled from Sandra's belt came savagely down. Hope shrieked in agony as the knife cut deep. Sandra groggily crawled to the two women, and pulled Deception from on top of Hope. The woman lay on the floor, the blade deep in her shoulder. She moaned in pain. Sandra pulled Hope across her lap, and cuddled her protectively, probing the dress to see how badly she was wounded. Suddenly they heard the pounding of footsteps outside. The voices were vague, their words indistinct. Sandra angrily reached for the rifle Hope still clutched to her in a death-like grip. Sandra couldn't wrench the gun loose; she then relaxed when she heard a familiar voice call out.

"Sandra. Where are you?" the congresswoman sighed thankfully as Stackit pounded through the door.

In the space of another heartbeat all her friends were there, Alex and Devron sporting wounds. Stackit had a graze across his cheek, but Justina was practically untouched, and what was more, she held onto a rope, with a thoroughly beaten and dispirited Anger tied up tightly.

* * *

Epilogue

Sandra sat beside the mound of freshly turned earth. She wept silently. She wanted to be able to save the woman so badly. The Original Sandra had trusted her to make this place safe again. It had taken only a few minutes to drag Anger down, and wish her away. Sandra looked at the gold watch in her hand; she turned it over, and through misty eyes read, 'My darling Sandra. May we never part, love Richard.' Sandra looked up and could see Hope climbing the small hill. Justina had bandaged the shoulder, and she now wore her arm in a sling. Sandra no longer thought of her as a clone or a copy. She was distinct individual with a mind, hopes and dreams of her own.

Hope carefully settled next to Sandra. "She truly loved you."

Sandra blinked. "I think it was you she loved. I know she was proud of you."

"Why did the Creator unlock the gate, and set the fire to attract the bad people?" She asked in anguish.

"Too many bad dreams. In the end she did what she thought was right. I think she knew how much you and Stackit cared for each other. I guess it was her way of giving you two a chance."

The two women sat in companionable silence. Hope leaned on Sandra's shoulder and sighed quietly. The congresswoman looked at the small gold watch she held in her hand, and leaning forward draped it over the small wooden cross Stackit had made.

"What now?" Sandra asked, as she rubbed her hands over her face.

Hope knew what she meant, and just shook her head. "I don't know. The Creator thought if she died that something would happen to this place."

"I wondered myself," Sandra said looking around.

Over the past two hours they had seen a few things happen. Another earthquake racked the area. They heard a massive rumble high in the mountains. It seemed as if this little world was coming apart.

"It could because one of us is still here. You were the Original Creator. Maybe this world is linked through you."

"Or you," Sandra said. "I have been thinking about both possibilities. What's going to happen when I leave? Will you be enough to hold this place together?" Sandra looked sideways at Hope.

"I would like to think I could. But I'm not sure of anything now," She said a catch in her voice. Obviously the death of the Original Sandra had hit her pretty hard.

"Why don't you come back with me, the others can as well?" Sandra said with inspiration.

"They are talking of that even now. When I left I don't think they want to. There are hundreds of other people, and beings in this world. Michael and Devron's honor won't allow them to be abandoned."

"Do you have to go back?" Hope asked as she burst into tears.

"I thought of staying, but if I don't go back, and the accident on earth still happens, then this place will never be formed."

"Do you think it will actually be formed anyway? From what I know of the Creator, she was scared of everything. You are one of the bravest women I know."

Sandra pulled Hope in close, and held her tightly as she broke down. She cried as if her heart was breaking.

"If I stay here, you won't have a chance with Stackit," Sandra joked lightly.

Hope blushed and hid deeper into Sandra's shoulder. "It is you he is smitten with."

"Don't sell yourself short. I have seen how you look at him, and I see how he looks at you when he doesn't think anyone is watching. His body language is of total love and devotion when he is around you."

Hope jerked her head up, her face shining. "Are you sure about that?"

She nodded, "Let's go down and see the others."

*   *   *

107

Stackit watched the two women come slowly down the hill, holding tight to each other's hand. "She's leaving."

The others stared at them too. "Can you be sure?" Justina asked.

Stackit nodded miserably. "Yeah, I'm sure."

He watched the injured woman walking with Sandra, and hope filled his heart. He had a future here even so.

The small group stood before the shimmering blue hole. Hope was as good as her word, and was able to open the rift. Sultan waited, saddled and plucking at the grass. She looked at the miniature pegasus. The horse seemed to know something was happening, and he didn't look happy. Sandra hugged him tight, and scratched his neck.

"Hope, can you take care of Rocky for me?" her voice strained with emotion.

"Who's Rocky?" Hope asked confused.

"He's a flying squirrel on a TV show…" she gave the creature one more scratch. "Never mind. Can you take care of him?"

"Of course, you know I will."

They all came forward, and stood in an awkward circle. Justina didn't know Sandra as well as the others, but she too was somber. Devron came up and bowed to her, smiling. She leaned forward and hugged him, he held her tightly in return.

"We wanted you to have this," he replied, his voice tight with emotion. He gave her a thick piece of rolled up parchment.

Sandra unrolled it, and the group stared back. They had been drawn in such incredible likeness they seemed as if they would start speaking.

"I do have a few talents that doesn't call for butchering men," Devron said lightly.

Sandra gave each a small gift. Devron got her binoculars, Justina was given her cowboy hat, Stackit, her rifle and the spare box of cartridges, Sandra gave her hunting knife to Michael. She stood before Hope, and carefully unlatched the locket from around her neck and solemnly put it over Hope's head.

Emotionally drained, each person looked miserable, as she took up Sultan's reins and made for the blue hole.

She paused briefly and turned. "Good luck"

They all waved mutely, and then Sandra stepped through. She quickly looked back to see what might happen through the gate, but all she saw was a blinding flash of light.

Sandra reached up, and unrolled the parchment; they all stared at her with happy smiling faces. She lingered watching the blue circle close. Sandra couldn't help but wonder what the flash of light meant.

"I'll never forget any of you, ever." With that she looped the reins over Sultan's head, and looked into the late afternoon sky. It was almost the exact time she had left. Sandra mounted, she wasn't sure what day it was, but it suddenly didn't matter. She turned the gelding and headed back to Black Lake and Richard.

* * *

Hope surfaced slowly; rough calloused hands were gently shaking her. Her eyes opened to look at Stackit. He breathed a sigh of relief, and hugged her tight. She looked at the sky above her. It was the most vibrant blue she had ever seen. She gasped in surprise.

"If you think that's cool, you should see this."

Stackit helped her stand, and the couple could see a small village, nestled in the valley between three hills. All the Sanctuaries of the other people were spaced around a small square with a fountain in the center. They turned at the sound of a feminine cry of surprise.

"Michael, is that you?" Justina squealed in delight.

She rushed to him, as he looked up bewildered. His bearded face broke into a smile as he scrambled to his feet, and gathered his wife to him. Devron looked up and smiled slightly, he knew now what Nimm Bare-ehth was preparing him for. He looked up into the sky and closed his eyes basking in the hot sun. He watched the other two couples and smiled. He bowed his head giving thanks to Nimm Bare-ehth, that he had a whole new world to explore. As he looked to the far horizon, he couldn't help but think of Sandra. He smiled, and standing slowly made his way to the little village.

The End

About the Author

Fantasy Writer

Hi all, this is K.D. Nielson ... and welcome to my .... mind.

I am a full time writer in search of a publisher, so I have to work at my day job to pay the bills. I have been writing and telling stories now for over 30 years.

Since the 11,000+ earthquakes here in Christchurch, I have been free to indulge in my greatest passion, telling stories, while the city starts to get back on its feet. I have drawn on my experiences these past months (seems like years) of awful earthquakes, the years serving as a prison officer, and my time in the US Navy as part of Operation Deep Freeze, making seven deployments to Antarctica. Yes, in spite of everything, I am still sane. I have drawn on my daily experiences in these jobs and the different facets of everyday life, as material for my books.

I have a wealth of intrigue, love, betrayal, war and heroic deeds just waiting for an avid reader. I have finished several books in the world I have created. They are just waiting to be discovered by that right someone, hopefully a publisher. All my books are available on Amazon through Kindle, and Createspace's print on demand.

I am married to a lovely English girl, a schoolteacher, and we have three sons, one which seems to keep coming back, kind of cramps my style. My wife has donated (sometimes gang pressed might be more like it) hours of her valuable time helping me with editing and reading manuscripts, and being very patient with all my questions, some of them might be, well … dumb.

I have also been working with a like-minded friend who is a fantasy fan and a very good writer in her own right. She is also a renowned artist and in conjunction with another project connected to my books, she is working on sketches of the characters and creatures of my world.

For more information on my books go to http://www.theworldsofkdnielson.com

Thank you for bearing with me while I rabbit on ... I challenge you, step into my mind ….you might like it so much ... you may not want to leave.

KD Nielson

For KD Nielson new novel

Ghost Dancer

in the

Tale of Menel Fenn

read on for preview

Two armored men circled the crouching dragon, the spade-shaped, black tail flicked back and forth. Two bodies lay a short distance away, one shriveled and burnt; the other had deep rents gouged into his armor as the wyvern held one razor sharp taloned claw on the body. The growl from the monster came deep within his throat, reaching all the way from its rumbling chest. When one of the fighters moved, the long serpentine neck turned so the horned head was able to follow its tormenter. The red eyes, full of hate and anger, fixed unblinkingly on the man. The long sword from the dead man at its feet, still deep in its neck, oozed blood over the ebony scales. The black tried to use its breath weapon. Each time the dragon inhaled, the creature blanched in pain. A roar of frustration burst from the grim jaws. The human on the off side, lunged and the blade bit deep behind the front leg. The tail stabbed lightening quick and found the gap between the chest plate and the helm. The blood spurted up the scaled tail. The dragon reared back on three legs and using the front claw, it pulled the bloodied blade free. It tried to follow the metal clad man, but the new wound hampered his movement. Unexpectedly, the dragon spun awkwardly, and dived between the large stone arches.

Suddenly the whole area erupted in a crescendo of cheering and stomping. The fighter turned and threw up his arms in a gesture of jubilant acceptance of the crowd's appreciation. He hefted his hands in the air repeatedly.

"Victory! Victory!" he yelled.

Rapidly the man turned at a new sound. He quickly saw the figure of a giant red-haired, bare-chested barbarian charging forward.

"Yeah! Die you bottomless pit scum!" the giant bellowed belligerently.

The fighter tried to bring up his sword. The battle-axe clanged onto the raising steel, shattering it. The hammering blow numbed the fighter's arm. The barbarian swung with the second axe, and rent the armor. With a gurgling sigh, the armored figure, slowly turned, blood running from both his mouth and across the axe blade, still embedded in his chest.

The crowd erupted in booing; the hisses and catcalls reaching a crescendo of indignation. The barbarian clenched the left hand in a fist and threw it upwards across the right arm, as he was jubilantly encouraged by the crowd's displeasure. His gestures infuriated the onlookers, surging en masse to their feet, shouting obscenities at the hairy man. His elegant blown kisses enraged them all the more. The barbarian, turned, bent over and pulled his pants down, baring his hairy buttocks. Then, with total disdain for the hecklers, he strode triumphantly back through the arch he had charged from.

The angry exclamations rose to a shattering pitch, echoing off the stone seating. The booing and hissing began to get more pronounced as objects were thrown into the arena. The lights through the two arches went out and a third lit up as a tall, distinguished looking man in his late forties, stepped into the arena. If one were to look closely, they would have been able to see the faint smile. The man was dressed in the rich robes of a merchant. The breeches and polished boots could be seen as he raised his hands for silence. The thousands of spectators around the arena ignored him. He looked around. The stone seats went back a good sixty feet up at a sharp angle, affording all the audience a reasonably good view. He turned slightly and his penetrating look took in the full arena. There must be three thousand ticket holders here. A good turn out. It was a shame about the rest of the empty seats.

He smiled a tight little movement. The 'unexpected' appearance of the barbarian couldn't have been better timed if he had planned it himself. He sighed slightly; Alrid would most likely want to renegotiate his commission. They would have to wait and see if his 'treachery' was able to bring more spectators tomorrow. If the empty seats were filled, the barbarian certainly would have earned a bonus, and being the shrewd business man he was, Alrid would be ready with hand extended. The crowd finally took notice of the man, who having been caught up in the crowd's passion, had by now almost yelled himself hoarse in spite of his resolve to stay

114

detached. With a carefully rehearsed introduction, the next combat was announced.

The dark-skinned man stood at the back, near the walkway along the top row. He had been there most of the day. The sultry hot sun burned his uncovered head. He rubbed his bristled jaw and massaged his haggard eyes, looking back over the five-foot high wall into the city beyond. He rapidly turned as he heard a woman screech. The crowd leapt to their feet and howled in hearty approval as the scantily clad woman was dragged down by the four foot tall tiger. She screamed, and the other two women in the arena stabbed the mauling animal with long spears. It was unsure whether the crowd roared, supporting the blood sports, or the ample well-endowed bare flesh the women displayed.

The watching man ignored the commotion in the sands below. He was a professional and as part of his job, he often waited great lengths of time under adverse conditions. But this time, he was getting impatient and sighed in frustration. He still hadn't seen his contact. The last event of the day was just finishing and the guards below were dragging out the three corpses as the tiger was lured back through an arch. As the crowd stood to leave, he spotted her. He grinned slightly, and loitered; waiting in the dim upper stands, now the sun had sunk from sight. He quickly made his way down to the sand, looking slowly for the woman. He vaguely could see someone deeper in the combat area, near the arches and swiftly moved after her. In his haste, he forgot his cardinal rule; never…ever let your guard down, allowing yourself to become distracted. He stopped briefly, and peered more intently into the dark. Suddenly he heard a growl, and a four foot tall tiger slinked into view. The great head, snarled, the yellow eyes glared at him. The cat crouched low to the ground, the white trimmed belly inches off the sand. The tail snapped back and forth, as if with a life of its own. He heard a rumble deep in its chest. The man froze, and in mind numbing terror turned to run. In seconds, the tiger was on him. The man's screams echoed off the stone walls and the catacomb tunnels under the spectator stands.

Three other men and the one woman watched the man's demise from the shadows. The woman had her arms bent back upward making her stand hunched forward on her tiptoes. From the looks on the two guard's faces, they didn't like manhandling her in this fashion. The third man portrayed a different demeanor entirely. He savored the screams of the tiger's victim, licking his lips. He closed his eyes and arched his head back in an almost erotic fashion; a faint moan escaping his parted mouth. The woman's struggles roused the stranger and for a brief instant, irritation flashed across his handsome face. He literally leapt to her side and savagely backhanded her. The man, tremendously strong, rocked her head. Once more he was in control and the peaceful, almost serene expression returned to his face. Spittle flew from her lips as a startled cry escaped her, the delicate, finely shaped eyes clenched in agony. The shock of the attack made her bite down on her lip, she whimpered as oozing blood welled thickly. She looked up desperately through hair strewn over her classically-shaped face, blood dripped from her nose, staining the pale blue bodice of her gown. She tried to pull back, and then sagged, hanging limply now as her legs betrayed her. The two thugs staggered under the sudden weight. They gripped her so tightly under her arms; she couldn't help but scramble with her nerveless feet to ease the terrible pain from her burning arms.

"Shhh, I want to hear the rest," he whispered sweetly.
The woman moaned in terror and tried to back away from him as he ran a finger down her chest. His fingers lingered by the exotic swelling of the bottom of her breasts, and she threw her head back and a whimpering moan escaped her. The stranger leaned forward and breathed deeply as his fingers danced lightly with a life of their own, tormenting her. By the time he turned back to the arena, the cries had stopped.

Two hours later the two timid heavies were replaced by a tall Northland woman and a solid muscular man. The woman was dressed in a simple halter made of skins and her loins were girdled by a second piece. She was over six feet tall and had coal black hair. Her chest covering only served to emphasize her abundant bust. The man was barefaced with long brown hair. He wore only leather breeches and soft knee high boots. They waited in the sands as the stranger knelt over the woman.

She looked radically different from the terrified woman who had witnessed the brutal mauling by the tiger. She was stretched out on the sand, her arms out to the sides, her feet together, tied to stakes in the sand. She wore nothing, her naked skin pale under the torchlight the man and woman carried. Her face had been cleaned and her injuries tended, there wasn't a mark on her. The woman lay on the sand with her honey colored hair carefully fanned out around her head, artistically arranged as a morbid halo. The stranger knelt beside her and with a small paintbrush carefully finished the elaborate patterns over her lithe body. Her mouth was gagged and she whimpered quietly. As he painted her breasts he lingered, his face near her neck savoring her anguish and humiliation. He kissed her softly on the graceful arch of her neck. A tear ran down from her tightly clenched eyes. She moaned in terror, her breasts heaving with emotion. The stranger stood watching her ineffective attempts to free herself. He knelt beside her and savored the rich aroma her body emitted. Carefully, so as not to smudge the markings on her body or muss the carefully arranged hair, he removed her gag.

"Targe, you and Adira, leave, lest you join her."
The two fled the sand. The staked-out woman watched despairingly as they hastily departed. Her gaze quickly shifted to the stranger as he slowly stood, he looked more like a snake slowly uncoiling.
"Please…for the love of everything holy … don't do this!" she choked.
He paused momentarily, as if her plea moved him. He laughed lightly and shook his head, whether in anger or pity, smelling the aromatic fragrance suddenly darkening the sand under her even as it was absorbed.
"Die well." He said softly with a lover's whisper.
With that he kissed her on the forehead. Then he left, leaving the last torch sputtering, stuck in the sand beside her.

After what seemed like an eternity, she actually opened her eyes and looked around. Suddenly she could hear the flutter of wings, and a woman appeared before her. She stood there in all her majestic glory. The long raven hair fluttered in an unseen breeze, like a knight's pennant. The deep vee cut gown was red, emphasizing her startlingly beautiful body, the tight bodice boldly displaying her lush fullness.

"Help...me..." pleaded the captive woman.

"Oh, I will." She cooed seductively.

Suddenly sharp teeth filled her mouth. The staked out woman screamed in utter terror, thrashing about desperately as the woman slowly knelt beside her. Drawing her head back, mouth wide-open, she plunged white teeth deep into the captive's neck. The blond haired woman's shrieks echoed hauntingly among the dark shadows, flickering along the torch lit wall. She strained at the bonds, actually loosening one stake, as she fought to be free. The dark-haired woman continued biting down. The torch briefly flared and in the dying burst of drifting sparks, the captive woman's heels drummed impotently in the sand beneath.

In the dark, the stranger leaned against the wall, hypnotized by the gruesome scene he was savoring. He closed his eyes and tilted his head back, letting all his senses absorb every detail. He licked his lips. Adira and the Targe could only cringe as they listened. The Northland woman bent over and tried to hide behind her upraised hands, as a small child would, she made the sign for the 'protection from evil' as the sounds slowly faded.

CPSIA information can be obtained at www.ICGtesting.com
Printed in the USA
LVOW05s2309190814

399907LV00028B/1053/P